Anonymous

The Shœmaker's Sic Holiday

By Thomas Dekker - Nach Einem Drucke Aus Dem Jahre 1618 Neu

Herausgegeben Von Hermann Fritsche

Anonymous

The Shœmaker's Sic Holiday
By Thomas Dekker - Nach Einem Drucke Aus Dem Jahre 1618 Neu Herausgegeben Von Hermann Fritsche

ISBN/EAN: 9783337294977

Printed in Europe, USA, Canada, Australia, Japan

Cover: Foto ©Andreas Hilbeck / pixelio.de

More available books at **www.hansebooks.com**

The Shœmaker's Holiday

or

The Gentle Craft.

Nach einem Drucke aus dem Jahre 1618
neu herausgegeben

von

Hermann Fritsche,

Lehrer am Gymnasium zu Thorn.

THORN, 1862.

Schnellpressendruck der Rathsbuchdruckerei.

The Shœmaker's Holiday

or

The Gentle Craft.

**With the humorous life of Simon Eyre,
Shœmaker and Lord Mayor of London.**

As it was acted before the Queen's most excellent Majesty
on New-year's day at night, by the right honourable
Earl of Nottingham, Lord High Admiral of
England, his servants.

At London,

printed for John Wright, and are to be sold at his shop at the
sign of the bible, without New-gate.

1610.

To all good fellows, professors of the gentle craft, of what degree soever.

Kind gentlemen and honest boon campanions, I present
you here with a merry conceited comedy, called „the shoemaker's holiday", acted by my Lord Admiral's players at a
Christmas-time, before the Queen's most excellent Majesty.
For the mirth and pleasant matter, by her Highness graciously
accepted, being indeed no way offensive. The argument of
the play I will set down in this epistle. Sir Hugh Lacy, Earl
of Lincoln, had a young gentleman of his own name, his near
kinsman, that loved the Lord Mayor's daughter of London; to
prevent and cross which love, the Earl caused his kinsman to
be sent Colonel of a company into France; who resigned his
place to another gentleman his friend, and came, disguised like
a dutch shoemaker, to the house of Simon Eyre in Towerstreet, who served the Lord Mayor and his household with
shoes. The merriments that passed in Eyre's house, his coming to be Mayor of London, Lacy's getting his love, and
other accidents, with two merry Three-men's Songs — take all
in good worth, that is well intended, for nothing is purposed
but mirth; mirth lengtheneth life, which, with all other bless-
ings, I heartily wish you. Farewell.

1*

The first Three-men's song.

Oh, the month of may, the merry month of may,
So frolick, so gay, and so green, so green, so green,
Oh and then did I unto my true love say:
Sweet Peg, thou shalt be my summer's queen.

Now the nightingale, the pretty nightingale,
The sweetest singer in all the forest quire,
Entreats thee, sweet Peggy, to hear thy true love's tale;
Lo! yonder she sitteth, her breast against a briar.

But oh! I spy the cuckoo, the cuckoo, the cuckoo;
See, where she sitteth; come away, my joy:
Come away, I prithee, I do not like, the cuckoo
Should sing where my Peggy and I kiss and toy.

Oh, the month of may, the merry month of may,
So frolick, so gay, and so green, so green, so green,
Oh and then did I unto my true love say:
Sweet Peg, thou shalt be my summer's queen.

The second Three-men's song.
This is to be sung at the latter end.

Cold's the wind, and wet's the rain,
　Saint Hugh, be our good speed:
Ill is the weather that bringeth no gain,
　Nor helps good hearts in need.
Trowl the bowl, the jolly nut-brown bowl,
　And here kind mate to thee:
Let 's sing a dirge for Saint-Hugh's soul,
　And down it merrily.
Down adown, hey down adown,
　Hey dery, dery, down adown! *(Close with the tenor boy.)*
Ho well done, to me let come,
　Ring compass, gentle joy.
Trowl the bowl ec. *(As often as there be men to drink.
At last, when all have drunk, this verse:)*
Cold's the wind, and wet's the rain,
　Saint Hugh, be our good speed:
Ill is the weather that bringeth no gain,
　Nor helps good hearts in need.

The Prologue,
as it was pronounced before the Queen's Majesty.

As wretches in a storm, expecting day,
With trembling hands, and eyes cast up to heaven,
Make prayers the anchor of their conquered hopes,

So we, dear goddess, wonder of all eyes,
Your meanest vassals, through mistrust and fear,
To sink into the bottom of disgrace
By our imperfect pastimes, prostrate thus
On bended knees, our sails of hope do strike,
Dreading the bitter storms of your dislike.
Since then — unhappy men! — our hap is such,
That to ourselves our selves no help can bring,
But needs must perish, if your saint-like ears,
Locking the temple, where all mercy sits,
Refuse the tribute of our begging tongues;
Oh grant, bright mirror of true chastity,
From those life-breathing stars, your sunlike eyes,
One gracious smile: for your celestial breath
Must send us life, or sentence us to death.

[Dramatis Personae.

The King.

Cornwall, a nobleman in attendance of the king.

Lord Lincoln.

Rowland Lacy } cousins to Lord Lincoln.
Askew

Lovell.

Dodger.

Sir Roger Otley, Lord Mayor of London.

Warner
Scott } citizens.
Hammon

Simon Eyre, a shoemaker.

Hodge
Firke
Rafe Damport } Eyre's journey-men.
Roger

A skipper.

Rose, daughter to Sir Roger.

Sibyl, her waiting-woman.

Margery, Eyre's wife.

Jane, Rafe's wife.

Boys, apprentices, soldiers, hunters, servants, etc.

The Scene is during the greater part of the play in London, sometimes at Oldford, a country-house near London, belonging to the Lord Mayor.]

A pleasant comedy of the gentle craft.

[Scene 1.

London, a Street.]

Enter Lord Mayor, Lincoln.

Lin. My Lord Mayor, you have sundry times
Feasted myself, and many courtiers more;
Seldom or never can we be so kind,
To make requital of your courtesy.
But leaving this — I hear, my cousin Lacy
Is much affected to your daughter Rose.

L. M. True, my good Lord, and she loves him so well,
That I mislike her boldness in the chase.

Lin. Why, my Lord Mayor, think you it then a shame
To join a Lacy with an Otley's name?

L. M. Too mean is my poor girl for his high birth;
Poor citizens must not with courtiers wed,
Who will in silks and gay apparel spend
More in one year, than I am worth by far.
Therefore your honour need not doubt my girl.

Lin. Take heed, mylord, advise you what you do,
A verier unthrift lives not in the world,
Than is my cousin; for I'll tell you what.
Tis now almost a year since he requested
To travel countries for experience.
I furnished him with coin, bills of exchange,
Letters of credit, men to wait on him,
Solicited my friends in Italy
Well to respect him; but to see the end:
Scant had he journeyed through half Germany
But all his coin was spent, his men cast off,
His bills embezzled, and my jolly coz,
Ashamed to shew his bankrupt presence here,
Became a shoemaker in Wittemberg;
A goodly science for a gentleman
Of such descent! Now judge the rest by this.
Suppose your daughter have a thousand pound:
He did consume [much] more in one half year;
And make him heir to all the wealth you have:
One twelve-month's rioting will waste it all.
Then seek, mylord, some honest citizen
To wed your daughter to.

L. M.   I thank your Lordship.
[*Aside:*] Well, fox, I understand your subtilty. —
[*Aloud:*] As for your nephew, let your lordship's eye
But watch his actions, and you need not fear,

For I have sent my daughter far enough:
And yet your cousin Rowland might do well,
Now he hath learned an occupation,
And yet I scorn to call him son in law.
Lin. Ay, but I have a better trade for him.
I thank his Grace: he hath appointed him
Chief Colonel of all those companies,
Mustered in London, and the shires about,
To serve his Highness in those wars of France.
See, where he comes! Lovell, what news with you?

Enter Lovell, Lucy and Askew.

Lov. Mylord of Lincoln, 't is his Highness' will,
That presently your cousin ship for France,
With all his powers; he would not for a million,
But they should land at Deep within four days.
Lin. Go, certify his Grace, it shall be done.
Now, cousin Lacy, in what for wardedness
Are all your companies?
Lacy.   All well prepared,
The men of Hertfordshire are at Mile-end;
Suffolk and Essex train in Tuttlefields;
The Londoners, and those of Middlesex,
All gallantly prepared in Finsbury,
With frolick spirits long for their parting hour.
L. M. They have their imprest, coats, and furniture,
And if it please your cousin Lacy come
To the Guildhall, he shall receive his pay,
And twenty pounds besides, [the which] my brethren
Will freely give him, to approve our loves
We bear unto mylord your uncle here.
Lacy. I thank your Honour.
Lin.   Thanks, my good Lord Mayor.
L. M. At the Guildhall we will expect your coming. *(Exit.)*
Lin. To approve your loves to me? No subtilty,
Nephew: that twenty pound he doth bestow
For joy to rid you from his daughter Rose.
But, cousins both, now here are none but friends,
I would not have you cast an amorous eye
Upon so mean a project as the love
Of a gay wanton painted citizen.
I know, this churl even in the height of scorn
Doth hate the mixture of his blood with thine.
I pray thee, do thou so; remember, coz,
What honourable fortunes wait on thee.
Entreat the King's love, which so brightly shines,
And gilds thy hopes. I have no heir but thee:

And yet not thee, if with a wayward spirit
Thou start from the true bias of my love.
Lacy. Mylord, I will, for honour, not desire
Of lands or livings, or to be your heir
So guide my actions in pursuit of France
As shall add glory to the Lacies' name.
Lin. Coz, for these words here 's thirty portuguese,
And, cousin Askew, there 's a few for you.
Fair honour in her loftiest eminence
Stays in France for you, till you fetch her thence.
Then, nephew, clap swift wings on your designs;
Be gone, be gone, make haste to the Guildhall.
There presently I'll meet you. Do not stay:
Where honour becomes, shame attends delay. *(Exit.)*
Ask. How gladly would your uncle have you gone!
Lacy. True, coz, but I'll o'erreach his policies.
I have some serious business for three days,
Which nothing, but my presence, can despatch.
You, therefore, cousin, with the companies
Shall haste to Dover; there I'll meet with you,
Or, if I stay past my prefixed time,
Away for France; we 'll meet in Normandy.
The twenty pounds my Lord Mayor gives to me
You shall receive and these ten portuguese,
Part of mine uncle's thirty, gentle coz.
Have care to our great charge. I know, your wisdom
Hath tried itself in higher consequence.
Ask. Coz, all myself am yours; yet have this care,
To lodge in London with all secrecy.
Our uncle Lincoln hath, besides his own,
Many a jealous eye, that in your face
Stares only to watch means for your disgrace.

*Enter Simon Eyre, his wife, Hodge, Firke, Jane, and
Rafe with a piece.*

Eyre. Leave whining, leave whining; away with this whimp-
ering, this puling, these blubbering tears, and these wet eyes.
I'll get thy husband discharged; I warrant thee, sweet Jane.
Go too.
Hodge. Master, here be the captains.
Eyre. Peace, Hodge; hushed, you knave; hushed!
Firke. Here be the cavaliers and the coronels, master.
Eyre. Peace, Firke; peace my fine Firke; stand by with
your pishery-pashery; away, I am a man of the best presence,
I'll speak to them, an they were popes. Gentlemen, captains,
colonels, commanders, brave men, brave leaders, may it please
you to give me audience. I am Simon Eyre, the mad shoe-

maker of Towerstreet; this wench with the mealy mouth is my wife, I can tell you; here's Hodge, my man and my foreman, here's Firke, my fine firking journeyman, and this is blubbered Jane. All we come to be suitors for this honest Rafe: keep him at home, and as I am a true shoemaker, and a gentleman of the gentle craft, buy spurs yourself, and I'll find you boots these seven years.

Wife. Seven years, husband!

Eyre. Peace, midriff, peace; I know, what I do; peace!

Firke. Truly, master cormorant, you shall do God good service to let Rafe and his wife stay together. She's a young new married woman; if you take her husband away from her a night, you undo her. She may beg in the day-time, for he's as good a workman at a prick and an awl, as any is in our trade.

Jane. Oh let him stay, else I shall be undone.

Firke. Ay, truly, she shall be laid at one side like a pair of old shoes else, and be occupied for no use.

Lucy. Truly, my friends, it lies not in my power.
The Londoners are pressed, paid and set forth
By the Lord Mayor; I cannot change a man.

Hodge. Why, then you were as good be a corporal, as a colonel, if you cannot discharge one good fellow; and I tell you true, I think you do more than you can answer, to press a man within a year and a day of his marriage.

Eyre. Well said, melancholy Hodge; grammercy, my fine foreman.

Wife. Truly, gentlemen, it were ill done for such as you, to stand so stiffly against a poor young wife, considering her case, she is new married. But let that pass: I pray, deal not roughly with her, her husband is a young man and but newly entered; but let that pass.

Eyre. Away with your pishery-pashery, your pols and your edipols; peace, Midas; silence, Cisly Bumtrinket, let your head speak.

Firke. Yea and the horns too, master.

Eyre. To soon, my fine Firke, to soon; peace, scoundrels; see you this man? Captains, you will not release him — well, let him go; he is a proper shot, let him vanish! Peace, Jane, dry up thy tears, they 'll make his powder dankish. Take him, brave men. Hector of Troy was an hackney to him; Hercules and Termagant scoundrels; prince Arthur's round table, by the Lord of Ludgate, n'er fed such a tall, such a dapper swordman; by the life of Pharaoh, a brave resolute swordman. Peace Jane! I say no more, mad knaves.

Firke. See, see, Hodge, how my master raves in commendations of Rafe.

Hodge. Rafe, th'art a gull, by this hand, an thou goest.
Ask. I am glad, good master Eyre, it is my hap
To meet so resolute a soldier:
Trust me, for your report and love to him,
A common slight regard shall not respect him.
Lacy. Is thy name Rafe?
Rafe. Yes, Sir.
Lacy. Give me thy hand.
Thou shalt not want, as I am a gentleman.
Woman, be patient; God, no doubt, will send
Thy husband safe again; but he must go,
His country's quarrel says: it must be so.
Hodge. Th' art a gull, by my stirrup, if thou doest not
go; I will not have strike thee thy gimlet into these weak
vessels; prick thine enemies, Rafe.

Enter Dodger.

Dodg. Mylord your uncle on the Towerhill
Stays with the Lord Mayor and the aldermen,
And doth request you, with all speed you may
To hasten thither.
Ask. Cousin, come, let 's go..
Lacy. Dodger, run you before, tell them we come. *(Exit
This Dodger is my uncle's parasite, Dodger.)*
The arrant'st varlet that e'er breathed on earth;
He sets more discord of a noble house
By one day's broaching in his pickthank tales,
Than can be salved again in twenty years,
And he, I fear, shall go with us to France,
To pry into our actions.
Ask. Therefore, coz,
It shall behove you to be circumspect.
Lacy. Fear not', good cousin. Rafe, hie to your colours.
(Lacy and Askew exeunt.)
Rafe. I must, because there is no remedy.
But, gentle master, and my loving dame,
As you have always been a friend to me,
So in my absence think upon my wife.
Jane. Alas, my Rafe.
Wife. She cannot speak for weeping.
Eyre. Peace, you cracked groats; you mustered tokens;
disquiet not the brave soldier. Go thy ways, Rafe.
Jane. Ay, ay, you bid him go; what shall I do,
When he is gone?
Firke. Why, be doing with me or my fellow Hodge, be
not idle.

Eyre. Let me see thy hand, Jane. This fine hand, this white hand, these pretty fingers must spin, must card, must work; work, you bumbast - cotton - candle - queen; work for your living. With a pox to you! Hold thee, Rafe, here's five sixpences for thee; fight for the honour of the gentle craft, for the gentlemen shoemakers, the courageous cordwainers, the flower of St. Martin's, the mad knaves of Bedlam, Fleetstreet, Towerstreet, and White-Chapel. Crack me the crowns of the french knaves; a pox on them, crack them; fight, by the Lord of Ludgate; fight, my fine boy.

Firke. Here, Rafe, here's two twopences, to carry into France; the third shall wash our souls at parting, for sorrow is dry. For my sake, firk the Baise-mon-culs.

Hodge. Rafe, I am heavy at parting, but here's a shilling for thee, god send thee to cram thy slop with French crowns and thy enemies' bellies with bullets.

Rafe. I thank you, master, and I thank you all.
[Now,] gentle wife, my loving, lovely Jane,
Rich men at parting give their wives rich gifts,
Jewels and rings, to grace their lily hands.
Thou knowest our trade makes rings for women's heels:
Here, take this pair of shoes cut out by Hodge,
Stitched by my fellow Firke, seamed by myself,
Made up and pinked with letters for thy name.
Wear them, my dear Jane, for thy husband's sake,
And every morning, when thou pull'st them on,
Remember me, and pray for my return.
Make much of them, for I have made them so,
That I can know them from a thousand mo.

Sound drum. Enter Lord Mayor, Lincoln, Lacy, Askew. Dodger, and Soldiers. They pass over the stage. Rafe falls in amongst them, Firke and the rest cry farewell etc, and so exeunt.

[Scene 2.
Oldford. A garden.]
Enter Rose alone, making a garland.

Rose. Here sit thou down upon this flowery bank,
And make a garland for thy Lacy's head.
These pinks, these roses, and these violets,
These blushing gillyflowers, these marigolds,
The fair embroidery of his coronet,
Carry not half such beauty in their cheeks,
As the sweet countenance of my Lacy doth.
Oh my most unkind father! Oh my stars!
Why lowered you so at my nativity,

To make me love, yet live robbed of my love?
Here as a thief am I imprisoned,
For my dear Lacy's sake, within those walls,
Which by my father's cost were builded up
For better purposes: here must I languish
For him that doth as much lament, I know,
Mine absence, as for him I pine in woe.

Enter Sibyl.

Sib. Good morrow, young mistress; I am sure you make that garland for me, against I shall be lady of the harvest.

Rose. Sibyl, what news at London?

Sib. None but good: my Lord Mayor, your father, and master Philpot your uncle, and master Scot your cousin and Mrs. Frigbottom by Doctor Commons, do all, by my troth, send you most hearty commendations.

Rose. Did Lacy send kind greetings to his love?

Sib. Oh yes, out of cry, by my troth, I scant knew him; here he wore a scarf, and here a scarf, here a bunch of feathers, and here precious stones and jewels, and a pair of garters: Oh monstrous, like one of your yellow silk courtains at home here in Oldford-house, here in master Bellymount's chamber. I stood at our door in Cornhill, looked at him, he at me; indeed spake to him, but he to me not a word; marry gip, thought I, with a wanion! He past by me as proud — marry foh! are you grown humorous, thought I? And so shut the door and in I came.

Rose. Oh Sibyl, how doest thou my Lacy wrong!
My Rowland is as gentle as a lamb,
No dove was ever half so mild as he.

Sib. Mild? Yea, as a bushel of stamped crabs; he looked up to me as sour as verjuice. Go thy ways, thought I; thou mayest be much in my gaskins, but nothing in my neather-stocks. This is your fault, mistress, to love him that loves not you. He thinks scorn to do, as he's done to; but if I were as you, I'd cry: go by Jeronimo, go by!

I'd set my old debts against my new dribblets,
And the hare's foot against the goose-giblets;
For if ever I sigh, when sleep I should take,
I pray God I may loose my maidenhead, when I wake.

Rose. Will my love leave me then and go to France?

Sib. I know not that, but I am sure, I see him stalk before the soldiers; by my troth, he is a proper man, but he is proper that proper doth. Let him go snick-up, young mistress.

Rose. Get thee to London and learn perfectly,
Whether my Lacy go to France or no:
Do this and I will give thee for thy pains

My cambrick apron and my romish gloves.
My purple stockings, and a stomacher.
Say, wilt thou do this, Sibyl, for my sake?
Sib. Will I, quoth a? at whose suit? by my troth, yes,
I'll go, a cambrick apron, gloves, and a pair of purple stockings
and a stomacher. I'll sweat in purple, mistress, for you, I'll
take any thing that comes a God's name. Oh rich! a cam-
brick apron! Faith, then have at up tails all, I'll go jiggy-
joggy to London and be here in a trice, young mistress.
Rose. Do so, good Sibyl. Mean time wretched I
Will sit and sigh for his lost company. *(Exeunt.)*

[Scene 3.

London. A Street.]

Enter Rowland Lacy like a dutch shoemaker.

Lacy. How many shapes have gods and kings devised
Thereby to compass their desired loves?
It is no shame for Rowland Lacy then,
To cloth his cunning with the gentle craft,
That, thus disguised, I may unknown possess
The only happy presence of my Rose.
For her have I forsook my charge in France,
Incurred the king's displeasure, and stirred up
Rough hatred in mine uncle Lincoln's breast.
Oh love, how powerful art thou, that canst change
High birth to bareness, and a noble mind
To the mean semblance of a shoemaker!
But thus it must be, for her cruel father
Hating the single union of our souls
Hath secretly conveyed my Rose from London,
To bar me of her presence; but I trust,
Fortune and this disguise will further me,
Once more to view her beauty, gain her sight:
Here in Towerstreet with Eyre the shoemaker,
Mean I a while to work; I know the trade;
I learned it, when I was in Wittemberg.
Then cheer thy hoping spirits, be not dismayed,
Thou canst not want, do Fortune what she can,
The gentle craft is living for a man. *(Exit.)*

[Scene 4.

An open yard before Eyre's house.]

Enter Eyre making himself ready.

Eyre. Where be these boys, these girls, these drabs, these
scoundrels? They wallow in the fat brewis of my bounty and

lick up the crums of my table, yet will not rise to see my walks cleansed: come out, you powder-beef-queens; what, Nan, what, Madge Mumble-crust, come out, you fat midriff-swag-belly whores, and sweep me these kennels, that the noisome filth offend not the noses of my neighbours. What, Firke, I say; what, Hodge, open my shop-windows; what, Firke, I say.

Enter Firke.

Firke. O master, is 't you that speak bandog and Bedlam this morning? I was in a dream and mused, what madman was got into the street so early: have you drunk this morning, that your throat is so clear?

Eyre. Ah, well said, Firke; well said, Firke. To work, my fine knave, to work! Wash thy face and thou 'lt be more blest.

Firke. Let them wash my face that will eat it, good master. Send for a housewife, if you will have my face cleaner.

Enter Hodge.

Eyre. Away, sloven! Avaunt, scoundrel! Good morrow, Hodge; good morrow, my fine fore-man.

Hodge. O master, good morrow; you 're an early stirrer. Here's a fine morning. Good morrow Firke. I could have slept this hour. Here 's a brave day toward.

Eyre. O, haste to work, my fine fore-man, haste to work.

Firke. Master, I am dry as dust to hear my fellow Hodge talk of fair weather: let us pray for good leather, and let clowns and ploughboys and those that work in the fields pray for brave days. We work in a dry shop, what care I, if it rain?

Enter Eyre's wife.

Eyre. How now, dame Margery, can you see to rise? Trip and go, call up the drabs, your maids.

Wife. See to rise? I hope, 't is time enough, 't is early enough for any woman, to be seen abroad. I marvel, how many wives in Towerstreet are up so soon. God's me, 't is not noon; here's a yawling.

Eyre. Peace Margery, peace, where's Cisly Bumtrinket, your maid? she has a privy fault; she farts in her sleep, call the quean up; if my men want shoe-thread, I'll swing her in a stirrup.

Firke. Yet that's but a dry beating; here's still a sign of drought.

Enter Lacy, singing.

Lacy. Der was een bore van Gelderland,
Frolick si byen;
He was als dronk, he cold niet stand,
Upsolee se byen;
Tap eens de cannekin,
Drink, schene mannekin!

Firke. Master, for my life, yonder 's a brother of the
gentle craft; if he bear not Saint Hugh's bones, I'll forfeit my
bones; he 's some uplandish workman; hire him, good master,
that I may learn some gibble-gabble, 't will make us work
the faster.

Eyre. Peace, Firke! A hard world! Let him pass, let him
vanish, we have journeymen enow. Peace, my fine Firke.

Wife. Nay, nay, you're best follow your man's counsel;
you shall see, what will come on't; we have not men enow,
but we must entertain every butterbox; but let that pass.

Hodge. Dame, for God, if my master follow your counsel,
he 'll consume little beef; he shall be glad of men, and he
can catch them.

Firke. Why, that he shall.

Hodge. Afore God, a proper man, and I warrant, a fine
workman; master, farewell; dame, adieu; if such a man as he
cannot find work, Hodge is not for you.   *(Offer to go.)*

Eyre. Stay, my fine Hodge.

Firke. Faith, an your foreman go, dame, you must take
a journey, to seek a new journeyman. If Hodge remove,
Firke follows; if Saint Hugh's bones shall not be set a work,
I may prick mine awl into the walls and go play: fare ye
well, master; god bye, dame.

Eyre. Tarry, my fine Hodge, my brisk foreman; stay,
Firke! peace, pudding-broth; by the Lord of Ludgate, I love
my men as my life; peace you gallimaufrey; Hodge, if he
want work, I'll hire him. One of you to him. Stay, he
comes to us.

Lacy. Goeden dach meester, end you¹²) fro oak.

Firke. Nails! If I should speak after him without drinking,
I should choke; and you friend oak, are you of the gentle
craft?

Lacy. Yaw, yaw, ich been den skoomaker.

Firke. Den skoomaker, quoth a; and hearken you, skoomaker, have you all your tools, a good rubbing pin, a good
stopper, a good dresser, your four sorts of awls, and your
two balls of wax, your paring knife, your hand- and thumb-
leathers, and good Saint-Hugh's bones to smooth up your
work?

Lacy. Yaw, yaw, be niet vor feard; ik hab all de dingen, for to mack skooes groot and clean.

Firke. Ha, ha! good master, hire him, he'll make me laugh so that I shall work more in mirth, than I can in earnest.

Eyre. Hear you, friend, have you any skill in the mistery of cordwainers?

Lacy. Ik weet niet, wat you seg, ick verstaw you niet.

Firke. Why, thus, man: [(*imitating by gesture a shoe-maker at work.*)] Ik verste you niet, quoth a.

[*Lacy.*] Yaw, yaw, ik can dat well doen.

Firke. Yaw, yaw; he speaks yawing like a Jack-daw, that gapes to be fed with cheese-curds. O, he'll give a villainous pull at a can of double beer. But Hodge and I have the vantage, because we are the eldest journeymen.

Eyre. What is thy name?

Lacy. Hans, Hans Meulter.

Eyre. Give me thy hand; thou art welcome. Hodge, entertain him, Firke, bid him welcome; come, Hans; run, wife, bid your maids, your trullibubs, make ready my fine men's breakfasts: to him, Hodge.

Hodge. Hans, th'art welcome; use thyself friendly, for we are good fellows; if not, thou shalt be fought with, wert thou bigger, than a giant.

Firke. Yea, and drunk with, wert thou Gargantua. My master keeps no cowards, I tell thee: ho, boy, bring him an heel-block, here's a new journeyman.

Enter Boy.

Lacy. O, ich wersto you, ich moet een halve dossen cans betalen: here, boy, nempt dis skilling, tap eens freelick.
                                            (Exit Boy.)

Eyre. Quick snipper-snapper, away Firke, scour thy throat, thou shalt wash it with Castilian liquor.

Enter Boy.

Come, my last of the fives, give me a can. Have to thee, Hans; here, Hodge; here Firke; drink you mad Greeks, and work like true Trojans, and pray for Simon Eyre, the shoemaker. Here, Hans, and th'art welcome.

Firke. Lo, dame, you would have lost a good fellow, that will teach us to laugh; this beer came hopping in well.

Wife. Simon, it is almost seven.

Eyre. Is 't so, dame clapper-dudgeon? Is 't seven a clock, and my men's breakfast not ready? Trip and go, you soused conger! Away? Come, you mad Hyperboreans; follow me, Hodge; follow me, Hans; come after, my fine Firke; to work, to work a while, and then to breakfast.   *(Exit.)*

Firke. Soft! Yaw, yaw, good Hans; though my master have no more wit, but to call you afore me, I am not so foolish, to go behind you, I being the elder journeyman.

(Exeunt.)

[Scene 5.

A field, near Oldford.]

Hallooing within. Enter Warner and Hammon, like hunters.

Ham. Cousin, beat every brake, the game's not far;
This way with winged feet he fled from death,
Whilst the pursuing hounds, scenting his steps,
Find out his highway to destruction.
Besides the miller's boy told me even now,
He saw him take soil, and he hallooed him,
Affirming him so embossed,
That long he could not hold.
War. If it be so,
'T is best, we trace these meadows by Oldford.

A noise of hunters within. Enter a boy.

Ham. How now, boy? Where 's the deer? speak, sawst
thou him?
Boy. O yea; I saw him leap through a hedge, and then over a ditch, then at my Lord Mayor's pale over he skipped me; and in he went me, and holla! the hunters cried, and there, boy! But there he is, a mine honesty.
Ham. Boy, god a mercy. Cousin let's away,
I hope, I shall find better sport to day.

[Scene 6.

Another part of the field.]

Hunting within. Enter Rose and Sibyl.

Rose. Why, Sibyl, wilt thou prove a forester?
Sib. Upon some, no, forester go by: no, faith, mistress, the deer came running into the barn, through the orchard and over the pale; I wot well, I looked as pale as a new cheese, to see him. But whip! says goodman Pinclose, up with his flail, and our Nick with a prong, and down he fell, and they upon him, and I upon them. By my troth, we had such sport; and in the end we ended him, his throat we cut, flayed him, unhorned him, and my Lord Mayor shall eat of him anon, when he comes. *(Horns sound within.)*

Rose. Hark, hark, the hunters come; you 're best take heed,
They have a saying to you for this deed.

Enter Hammon, huntsmen and boy.

Ham. God save you, fair ladies.
Sib.   Ladies, o gross!
Warn. Came not a buck this way?
Rose.   No, but two does.
Ham. And which way went they? Faith, we'll hunt at those.
Sib. At those? Upon some, no: when, can you tell?
War. Upon some, I.
Sib.   Good Lord!
War.   Wounds! Then, farewell!
Ham. Boy, which way went he?
Boy.   This way, sir, he ran.
Ham. This way, he ran indeed, fair mistress Rose;
Our game was lately in your orchard seen.
War. Can you advise, which way he took his flight?
Sib. Follow your nose, his horns will guide you right.
War. Thou'rt a mad wench.
Sib.   O rich!
Rose.   Trust me, not I.
It is not like, that the wild forest deer
Would come so near to places of resort.
You are deceived, he fled some other way.
War. Which way, my sugar-candy, can you show?
Sib. Come up, good honeysops, upon some, no.
Rose. Why do you stay, and not pursue your game?
Sib. I'll hold my life, their hunting nags are lame.
Ham. A deer more dear is found within this place.
Rose. But not the deer, Sir, which you had in chase.
Ham. I chased the deer, but this deer chaseth me.
Rose. The strangest hunting that I ever see.
But where's your park? (*She offers to go away.*)
Ham.   'T is here; o, stay!
Rose. Impale me, [sir,] and then I will not stray.
War. They wrangle, wench; we are more kind than they.
Sib. What kind of heart is that, deer heart, you seek?
War. A hart, dear heart.
Sib.   Who ever saw the like?
Rose. To loose your hart, is 't possible, you can?
Ham. My heart is lost.
Rose.   Alack, good gentleman.
Ham. This poor lost heart, would I wish, migt you find.
Rose. You, by such luck, might prove your heart a hind.
Ham. Why, luck had horns, so have I heard some say.
Rose. Now, God, an 't be his will, send luck unto your way.

Enter Lord Mayor, and servants.

L. M. What, Mr. Hammon? Welcome to Oldford.
Sib. God's pittikins, hands off, sir! Here's mylord.
L. M. I hear, you had ill luck, and lost your game.
Ham. 'T is true, mylord.
L. M.   I'm sorry for the same.
What gentleman is this?
Ham.   My brother-in-law.
L. M. You 're welcome both; sith fortune offers you
Into my hands, yon shall not part from hence,
Until you have refreshed your wearied limbs.
Go, Sibyl, cover the board! You shall bo guest
To no good fare, but even a hunter's feast.
Ham. I thank your lordship. Cousin, on my life,
For our lost venison, I shall find a wife.   *(Exeunt.)*
L. M. In, gentlemen; I'll not be absent long.
This Hammon is a proper gentleman,
A citizen by birth, fairly allied.
How fit an husband were he for my girl!
Well, I will in and do the best I can,
To match my daughter to this gentleman.   *(Exit.)*

[Scene 7.

A room in Eyre's house.]

Enter Lacy, Skipper, Hodge and Firke.

Skip. Ik sal you wat seggen, Hans; dis skip dat comen
from Candy, is all voll, by Got's sacrament, van sugar, civet,
almond, cambric end alle dingen, towsand, towsand dingen.
Nempt it, Hans; nempt it for u meester. Daer be de bills van
laden. Your meester Simon Eyre sal hae good copen. Wat
seggen you, Hans?

Firke. Wat seggen de reggen de copen, slopen — laugh,
Hodge, laugh!

Lacy. Mine liever broder Firke, bringt meester Eyre lot
det sign vn swannekin. Dare sal you find dis skipper and
me. Wat seggen you, broder Firke? Doot it, Hodge. Come,
skipper.   *(Exeunt.)*

Firke. Bring him, qd. you? Here's no knavery, to bring
my master, to buy a ship, worth the lading of 2 or 3 hundred
thousand pounds. Alas, that's nothing; a bauble, Hodge.   ·

Hodge. The truth is, Firke, that the merchant owner of
the skip dares not show his head, and therefore this skipper,
that deals for him, for the love he bears to Hans, offers my
master Eyre a bargain in the commodities. He shall have a

2*

reasonable day of payment; he may sell the wares by that time and be an huge gainer himself.

Firke. Yea, but can my fellow Hans lend my master twenty Propentines as an earnest penny?

Hodge. Portuguese thou wouldst say; here they be Firke. Hark, they jingle in my pocket like S. Mary-Queries bells.

Enter Eyre and his wife.

Firke. Mum, here comes my dame and my master: she'll scold, on my life, for loitering this monday; but all's one, let them all say what they can: Monday's our holiday. [(*Sings.*)]

Wife. You sing, Sir Sauce, but I beshrew your heart, I fear for this your singing we shall smart.

Firke. Smart for me, dame? why, dame, why?

Hodge. Master, I hope you'll not suffer my dame, to take down your journeyman.

Firke. If she take me down, I'll take her up, yea, and take her down too, a button-hole lower.

Eyre. Peace Firke; not I, Hodge; by the life of Pharao, by the Lord of Ludgate, by this beard, every hair of which I value at a king's ransom, she shall not meddle with you. Peace, you bumbast-cotton-candle-queen; away, queen of clubs, quarrel not with me and my men, with me and my fine Firke; I'll firk you, if you do.

Wife. Yea, yea, man; you may use me, as you please. But let that pass.

Eyre. Let it pass, let it vanish away: peace, am I not Simon Eyre? are not these my brave men? brave shoemakers, all gentlemen of the gentle craft? Prince am I none, yet am I nobly born, as being the sole son of a shoemaker. Away, rubbish! vanish! melt, melt like kitchin-stuff!

Wife. Yea, yea, 't is well. I must be called rubbish, kitchin-stuff, for a sort of knaves.

Firke. Nay, dame, you shall not weep and wail in woe for me: master, I'll stay no longer, here's an eventory of my shop-tools. Adieu, master; Hodge, farewell.

Hodge. Nay, stay, Firke; thou shalt not go alone.

Wife. Pray, let them go; there be moe maids than Mawkin, more men than Hodge, and more fools than Firke.

Firke. Fools? Nails, if I tarry now, I would my guts might be turned to shoe-thread.

Hodge. And if I stay, I pray God, I may be turned to a Turk, and set in Finsbury for boys to shoot at: come, Firke.

Eyre. Stay, my fine knaves, you arms of my trade, you pillars of my profession. What, shall a little-tattle word make you forsake Simon Eyre? Avaunt, kitchin-stuff! Rip, you brown-bread tanniking, out of my sight! move me not! Have not I ta'en you from selling tripes in Eastcheap, and set you in my shop, and made you hailfellow with Simon Eyre, the shoemaker? And now do you deal thus with my journeymen? Look, you powder-beef-queen, on the face of Hodge? Here's a face for a lord.

Firke. And here's a face for any lady in Christendom.

Eyre. Rip, you chitterling! Avaunt, boy, bid the tapsters of the Boar's-Head fill me a dozen cans of beer for my journeymen.

Firke. A dozen cans? O brave, Hodge, now I'll stay.

Eyre. [*In a low voice to the boy:*] An the knave fills any more, than two, he pays for them. [*Exit Boy. Loud.*] A dozen cans of beer for my journeymen. [*Reenter Boy.*] Here, you mad Mesopotamians, wash your livers with this liquor. Where be the odd ten? No more, Madge, no more; well said; drink and to work. What work doest thou, Hodge? What work?

Hodge. I am a making a pair of shoes for my Lord Mayor's daughter, mistress Rose.

Firke. And I a pair of shoes for Sibyl, mylord's maid; I deal with her.

Eyre. Sibyl? fie, defile not thy fine workmanly fingers with the feet of kitchin-stuff and basting ladles. Ladies of the court, fine ladies, my lads, commit their feet to apparelling. Put gross work to Hans, yark and scam, yark and seam.

Firke. For yarking and seaming let me alone, an I come to't.

Hodge. Well, master, all this is from the bias. Do you remember the ship, my fellow Hans told you of? The skipper and he are both drinking at the swan. Here be the portuguese to give earnest. If you go through with it, you cannot choose but be a lord at least.

Firke. Nay, dame, if my master prove not a lord, and you a lady, hang me.

Wife. Yea, like enough, if you may loiter and tipple thus.

Firke. Tipple, dame? no, we have been bargaining with Skellum Skanderbag: can you Dutch spreaken for a ship of silk cypress, laden with sugar-candy?

Eyre. Peace, Firke; silence, Tittle-tattle. Hodge, I'll go through with it, here's a seal-ring, and I have sent for a guarded gown and a damask cassock. (*Enter the boy with a velvet coat and an alderman's gown. Eyre puts it on.*) See, where it comes; look here, Maggy; help me, Firke; apparel me, Hodge; silk and satin, you mad Philistines, silk and satin.

Firke. Ha, ha, my master will be as proud as a dog in a doublet, all in beaten damask and velvet.

Eyre. Softly, Firke, for rearing of the nap, and wearing thread-bare my garment. How doest thou like me, Firke? How do I look, my fine Hodge?

Hodge. Why, now you look like yourself, master; I warrant you, there's few in the city, but will give you the wall and come upon you with the right worshipful.

Firke. Nails, my master looks like a thread-bare cloak new turned and dressed. Lord, Lord, to see what good raiment doth! Dame, dame, are you not enamoured?

Eyre. How sayest thou, Maggy, am I not brisk? am I not fine?

Wife. Fine? By my troth, sweet heart, very fine! By my troth, I never liked thee so well in my life, sweet heart. But let that pass; I warrant, there be many women in the city, have not such handsome husbands, but only for their apparel; but let that pass, too.

Enter Hans and Skipper.

Hans. Godden day, meester; dis be de skipper, dat heb de skip van merchandice; de commodity been good; nempt it meester, nempt it.

Eyre. God a mercy, Hans; welcome, skipper; where lies this skip of merchandize?

Skip. De skip been in rouere; dor be van sugar, civet, almonds, cambric and a towsand, towsand tings — Got's sacrament, nempt it meester: ye sal heb good copen.

Firke. To him, master! O sweet master! O sweet wares! Prunes, almonds, sugar-candy, carrot-roots, turnips — o brave fatting meat! Let not a man buy a nutmeg, but yourself.

Eyre. Peace, Firke! Come, skipper; I'll go aboard with you. Hans, have you made him drink?

Skip. Yaw, yaw, ick heb veal gedrunke.

Eyre. Come, Hans, follow me. Skipper, thou shalt have my countenance in the city.

Firke. Yaw, heb veal gedrunke, quoth a: they may well be called butterboxes, when they drink fat veal, and thick beer too. But come, dame, I hope you 'll chide us no more.

Wife. No, faith, Firke; no, perdy, Hodge. I do feel honour creep upon me, and which is more, a certain rising in my flesh; but let that pass.

Firke. Rising in your flesh do you feel, say you? Why, you may be with child; but why should not my master feel a rising in his flesh, having a gown and a gold ring on? But you are such a shrew, you 'll soon pull him down.

Wife. Ha, ha! prithee, peace! Thou makest my worship laugh; but let that pass. Come, I'll go in; Hodge, prithee, go before me; Firke follow me.

Firke. Firke doth follow; Hodge, pass out in state. *(Exeunt.)*

[Scene 8.

London. A room in Lincoln's house.]

Enter Lincoln and Dodger.

Lin. How now, good Dodger, what's the news in France?
Dodg. Mylord, upon the eighteenth day of May
The French and English were prepared to fight;
Each side with eager fury gave the sign
Of a most hot encounter; five long hours
Both armies fought together. At the length
The lot of victory fell on our sides.
Twelve thousand of the Frenchmen that day died,
Four thousand English, and no man of name
But captain 'Hyam and young Ardington,
Two gallant gentlemen, I knew them well.
Lin. But, Dodger, prithee, tell me, in this fight
How did my cousin Lacy bear himself?
Dodg. Mylord, your cousin Lacy was not there.
Lin. Not there?
Dodg. No, my good lord.
Lin. Sure, thou mistakest.
I saw him shipped, and a thousand eyes beside
Were witness of the farewells which he gave,
When I with weeping eyes bid him adieu:
Dodger, take heed.
Dodg. Mylord, I am advised,
That what I speak, is true: to prove it so,
His cousin Askew, that supplied his place,
Sent me for him from France, that secretly
He might convey him thither.
Lin. Is't even so?
Dares he so carelessly venture his life,
Upon the indignation of a king?
Hath he despised my love, and spurned those favours,
Which I with prodigal hand poured on his head?
He shall repent his rashness with his soul;
Since of my love he makes no estimate,
I'll make him wish, he had not known my hate.
Thou hast no other news?
Dodg. None else, mylord.
Lin. None worse I know thou hast: procure the king
To crown his giddy brows with ample honours,
Send him chief-colonel, and all my hope
Thus to be dashed? But 't is in vain to grieve,
One evil cannot a worse [one] relieve.
Upon my life, I have found out this plot;
The old dog Love that fawned upon him so;

Love to that puling girl, his fair-cheeked Rose,
The Lord Mayor's daughter, hath distracted him,
And in the fire of that love's lunacy
Hath he burnt up himself, consumed his credit,
Lost the king's love, yea, and I fear, his life,
Only to get a wanton to his wife:
Dodger, it is so.

Dodg.   I fear so, my good lord.

Lin. It is so — nay, sure, it cannot be.
I am at my wit's end, Dodger.

Dodg.   Yea, mylord.

Lin. Thou art acquainted with my nephew's haunts;
Spend this gold for thy pains; go, seek him out;
Watch at mylord Mayor's; there, if he live,   .
Dodger, thou shalt be sure, to meet with him:
Prithee, be diligent. — Lacy, thy name
Lived once in honour, [is] now dead in shame. —
Be circumspect.   *(Exit.)*

Dodg.   I warrant you, mylord *(Exit.)*

[Scene 9.

London. A room in the Lord Mayor's house.]

Enter Lord Mayor and Muster Scot.

L. M. Good master Scot, I have been bold with you,
To be a witness to a wedding knot,
Betwixt young master Hammon and my daughter.
O, stand aside; see, where the lovers come. [*Taking him
aside.*]

Enter Hammon and Rose.

Rose. Can it be possible, you love me so?
No, no, within those eye-balls I espy
Apparent likelihoods of flattery.
Pray now, let go my hand.

Ham.   Sweet mistress Rose,
Misconstrue not my words, nor misconceive
Of my affection, whose devoted soul
Swears, that I love thee dearer than my heart.

Rose. As dear as your own heart? I judge it right.
Men love their hearts best, when they 're out of sight.

Ham. I love you by this hand.

Rose.   Yet hands off now:
If flesh be frail, how weak and frail's your vow?

Ham. Then by my life I swear.

Rose. Then do not brawl;
One quarrel looseth wife and life and all.
Is not your meaning thus?
Ham. In faith, you jest.
Love loves to sport, therefore leave love, you 're best.
L. M. What? square they, master Scot?
Scott. Sir, never doubt,
Lovers are quickly in and quickly out.
Ham. Sweet Rose, be not so strange in fancying me.
Nay, never turn aside, shun not my sight.
I am not grown so fond, to fond my love
On any that shall quit it with disdain;
If you will love me, so; if not, farewell.
L. M. [(*stepping forth*)] Why, how now, lovers, are
you both agreed?

Ham. Yes, faith, mylord.
L. M. 'T is well, give me your hand
Give me yours, daughter. How now, both pull back!
What means this, girl?
Rose. I mean to live a maid.
Ham. (*Aside.*) But not to die one; pause, ere that be said.
L. M. Will you still cross me, still be obstinate?
Ham. Nay, chide her not, mylord, for doing well.
If she can live an happy virgin's life,
'T is far more blessed than to be a wife.
Rose. Say, sir, I cannot: I have made a vow,
Whoever be my husband, 't is not you.
L. M. Your tongue is quick; but, Mr. Hammon, know,
I bad you welcome to another end.
Ham. What would you have me pule, and pine, and pray
With „lovely lady“, „mistress of my heart“,
„Pardon your servant“, and the rimer play
Railing on Cupid and his tyrant's-dart?
Or shall I undertake some martial spoil,
Wearing your glove at tourney and at tilt,
And tell how many gallants I unhorsed —
Sweet, will this please you?
Rose. Yes, when will begin?
What, love-rhymes, man? Fie on that deadly sin!
L. M. If you will have her, I'll make her agree.
Ham. Enforced love is worse than hate to me.
[(*Aside.*)] There is a wench keeps shop in the old change,
To her will I; it is not wealth I seek:
I have enough; and will prefer her love
Before the world. [(*Loud*)] My good Lord Mayor, adieu!
Old love for me, I have no luck with new. (*Exit.*)

L. M. Now, mammet, you have well behaved yourself,
But you shall curse your coyness, I if live:
Who 's within there?

Enter Sibyl.

See, you convey your mistress
Straight to th' Oldford. — I'll keep you strait enough;
Fore God! I would have sworn, the puling girl
Would willingly accepted Hammon's love;
But banish him, my thoughts! Go, minion, in. (*Exeunt*
Rose and Sibyl.)
Now tell me, master Scott, would you have thought
That master Simon Eyre, the shoemaker,
Had been of wealth to buy such merchandize?
Scott. 'T was well, mylord, your honour and myself
Grew partners with him, for your bills of lading
Shew that Eyre's gains in one commodity
Rise at the least to full three thousand pound
Besides like gain in other merchandize.
L. M. Well, he shall spend some of his thousands now,
For I have sent for him to the Guildhall.

Enter Eyre.

See, where he comes, — good morrow, master Eyre.
Eyre. Poor Simon Eyre, mylord, your shoemaker.
L. M. Well, well, it likes yourself to term you so.

Enter Dodger.

Now, Mr. Dodger, what's the news with you?
Dodg. I 'd gladly speak in private to your honour
L. M. You shall, you shall. Master Eyre and Mr. Scott,
I have some business with this gentleman;
I pray, let me entreat you to walk before
To the Guildhall, I'll follow presently.
Master Eyre, I hope ere noon to call you sheriff.
Eyre. I would not care, mylord, if you might call me king
of Spain. Come, master Scott. [(*Exeunt Eyre and Scott.*)]
L. M. Now, master Dodger, what's the news you bring?
Dodg. The earl of Lincoln by me greets your Lordship
And earnestly requests you, if you can,
Inform him, where his nephew Lacy keeps.
L. M. Is not his nephew Lacy now in France?
Dodg. No, I assure your Lordship, but disguised
Lurks here in London.
L. M. London? Is 't even so?
It may be; but, upon my faith and soul,

I know not where he lives, or whether he lives.
So tell mylord of Lincoln. Lurk in London?
Well, master Dodger, you perhaps may start him.
Be but the means to rid him into France,
I'll give you a dozen angels for your pains,
So much I love his honour, hate his nephew;
And, prithee, so inform thy lord from me.
Dodg. I take my leave.   *(Exit Dodger.)*
L. M.   Farewell, good Mr. Dodger.
Lacy 's in London, I dare pawn my life;
My daughter knows thereof, and for that cause
Denied young master Hammon in his love.
Well, I am glad I sent her to Oldford. —
God's Lord! 't is late; to Guildhall I must hie:
I know my brethern lack my company.   *(Exit.)*

Scene 10.

London. A room in Eyre's house.]

Enter Firke, Eyre's wife, Hans and Roger.

Wife. Thou goest too fast for me, Roger. O, Firke!
Firke. Why, forsooth.
Wife. I pray thee, run — do you hear? — run to Guild-hall, and learn, if my husband, Mr. Eyre, will take that worshipful vocation of Mr. Sheriff upon him. Hie thee, good Firke.
Firke. Take it? Well, I go; an he should not take it, Firke swears to forswear him. Yes, forsooth, I go to Guildhall.
Wife. Nay, when? Thou wilt make me melancholy.
Firke. God forbid, your Worship should fall into that humour; I run.   *(Exit.)*
Wife. Let me see now Roger and Hans.
Rog. Why, forsooth, dame — mistress I should say, but the old term so sticks to the roof of my mouth, I can hardly lick it off.
Wife. Even what thou will, good Roger; dame is a fair name for any honest christian; but let that pass. How doest thou, Hans?
Hans. Me tanck you, vro.
Wife. Well, Hans and Roger, you see, God hath blessed your master, and, perdy, if ever he come to be Mr. Sheriff of London, (as we are all mortal), you shall se, I will have some odd thing or other in a corner for you; I will not be your back-friend, but let that pass; Hans, pray thee, lie my shoe.
Hans. Yaw, ik sal, vro.
Wife. Roger, thou knowest the length of my foot; as it is none of the biggest, so I thank God, it is handsome enough;

prithee, let me have a pair of shoes made; cork, good Roger, wooden heels, too.

Hodge. You shall.

Wife. Art thou acquainted with never a fardingale-maker, nor a french-hood-maker? I must enlarge my bum, ha, ha, ha! How shall I look in a hood, I wonder! perdy, oddly, I think.

Rog. As a cat out of a pillory; very well, I warrant you, mistress.

Wife. Indeed, all flesh is grass; and Roger, canst thou tell, where I may buy a good hair?

Rog. Yes, forsooth, at the poulterer's in Gracious-street.

Wife. Thou art on ungracious wag; perdy I mean a false hair for my periwig.

Rog. Why mistress, the next time, I cut my beard, you shall have the shavings of it; but mine are all true hair.

Wife. It is very hot, I must get me a fan or else a mask.

Rog. So you had need to hide your wicked face.

Wife. Fie upon it, how costly this world's calling is; perdy, but that it is one of the wonderful works of God, I would not deal with it. Is not Firke come yet? Hans, be not so sad, let it pass and vanish, as my husband's worship says.

Hans. Ik bin vrolick, lot see you so.

Rog. Mistress, wilt thou drink a pipe of tobacco?

Wife. O fie upon it, Roger. Perdy, these filthy tobacco-pipes are the most idle slavering baubles, that ever I felt: out upon it! God bless us, men look not like men that use them.

Enter Rafe, being lame.

Rog. What, fellow Rafe! Mistress, look here! Jane's husband! Why, how now, lame? Hans make much of him, he's a brother of our trade, a good workman and a tall soldier.

Hans. You be welcome, broder.

Wife. Perdy, I knew him not. How doest thou, good Rafe? I am glad to see thee well.

Wife. I would God, you saw me, dame, as well,
As when I went from London into France.

Wife. Trust me, I am sorry, Rafe, to see thee impotent. Lord, how the wars have made him sun-burnt! The left leg is not well; 't was a fair gift of God, the infirmity took not a little higher, considering thou camest from France; but let that pass.

Rafe. I'm glad to see you well and I rejoice
To hear that God hath blessed my master so
Since my departure.

Wife. Yea, truly, Rafe, I thank my maker; but let that pass.

Rog. And, sirrah Rafe, what news, what news in France?

Rafe. Tell me, good Roger, first, what news in England?
How does my Jane? When didst thou see my wife?
Where lives my poor heart? She'll be poor indeed,
Now I want limbs to get whereon to feed.
  Rog. Limbs? Hast thou not hands, man? Thou shalt
never see a shoemaker want bread, though he have but three
fingers on a hand.
  Rafe. Yet all this while I hear not of my Jane.
  Wife. O Rafe, your wife, — perdy, we know not, what's
become of her: she was here a while, and because she was
married, grew more stately than became her; I checked her,
and so forth, and away she flung, never returned, nor said
bih nor bah! And Rafe, you know, ka me, ka thee; and so as
I tell ye. Roger, is not Firke come yet?
  Rog. No, forsooth.
  Wife. And so indeed we heard not of her, but I hear
she lives in London: but let that pass. If she had wanted,
she might have opened her case to me or my husband, or to
any of my men. I am sure, there is not any of them, perdy,
but would have done her good to his power. Hans, look, if
Firke be come.
  Hans. Yaw, ik sal, vro.   *(Exit Hans.)*
  Wife. And so as I said: but Rafe, why doest thou weep?
Thou knowest not that naked we came out of our mother's
womb, and naked we must return, and therefore thank God
for all things.
  Rog. No, faith'; Jane is a stranger here, but Rafe pull
up a good heart, I know thou hast one. Thy wife, man, is in
London; one told me, he saw her a while ago very brave
and neat; we 'll ferret her out, an London hold her.
  Wife. Alas, poor soul, he's overcome with sorrow; he
does but, as I do, weep for the loss of any good thing: but
Rafe, get thee in, call for some meat and drink, thou shalt
find me worshipful towards thee.
  Rafe. I thank you, dame; since I want limbs and lands
I'll trust to God, my good friends, and my hands. *(Exit.)*

Enter Hans and Firke, running.

  Firke. Run, good Hans! O, Hodge, o mistress! Hodge,
heave up thine ears; mistress, smug up yonr looks; on with
your best apparel; my master is chosen, my master is called,
nay, condemned by the cry of the country, to be sheriff of the
City, for this famous year now to come. And time now being,
a great many men in black gowns were asked for their voices
and their hands, and my master had all their fists about his
ears presently and they cried: ay, ay, ay, ay! And so I came
away —

Wherefore without all other grieve
I do salute you, mistress shrieve.

Hans. Yaw, my meester is de gool man, de shrieve.

Rog. Did not I tell you, mistress? Now I may boldly say: Good morrow to your Worship.

Wife. Good morrow, good Roger. I thank you, my good people all. Firke, hold up thy hand: here's a three penny-piece for thy tidings.

Firke. 'T is but three halfpence, I think: yet 't is three-pence, I smell the rose.

Hodge. But, mistress, be ruled by me, and do not speak so pulingly.

Firke. 'T is her worship speaks so and not she. No, faith, mistress, speak me in the old key.

Wife. To it, Firke! There, good Firke! Ply your business, Hodge! Hodge, with a full mouth: I'll fill your bellies with good cheer, till they cry twang.

Enter Simon Eyre, wearing a gold-chain.

Hans. See, mine liever broder, here compt my meester.

Wife. Welcome home, master shrieve; I pray God continue you in health and wealth.

Eyre. See here, my Maggy, a chain, a gold-chain for Simon Eyre; I shall make thee a lady; here's a french hood for thee; on with it, on with it! Dress thy brows with this flap of a shoulder of mutton, to make thee look lovely. Where be my fine men? Roger, I'll make over my shop and tools to thee; Firke, thou shalt be the foreman; Hans, thou shalt have an hundred for twenty. Be as mad knaves, as your master Sim Eyre hath been, and you shall live to be sheriffs of London. How doest thou like me, Margery? Prince am I none, yet am I princely born. Firke, Hodge, Hans!

All three. Ay, forsooth, what says your Worship, master sheriff?

Eyre. Worship and honour, ye babylonian knaves, for the gentle craft: — but, I forgot myself, I am bidden by my Lord Mayor to dinner to Oldford; he 's gone before, I must after. Come, Madge, on with your trinkets: now, my true Trojans, my fine Firke, my dapper Hodge, my honest Hans, some device, some odd crotchets, some morris, or such like, for the honour of the gentlemen shoemakers. Meet me at Oldford, you know my mind: come, Madge, away; shut up the shop, knaves, and make holiday.

([*Eyre and his wife*] *exeunt.*)

Firke. O rare! O brave! Come, Hodge; follow me, Hans; We will be with them for a Morris dance. *(Exeunt.)*

[Scene 11.

Oldford. A room.]

Enter Lord Mayor. Eyre, his wife in a french hood,
[Rose] Sibyl and other servants.

L. M. Trust me, you are as welcome to Oldford, as myself.
Wife. Truly, I thank your Lordship.
L. M. 'Would, our bad cheer were worth the thanks you give.
Eyre. Good cheer, my Lord Mayor, fine cheer, a fine
house, fine walls, all fine and neat.
L. M. Now, by troth, I'll tell thee, master Eyre,
It does me good and all my brethren, [too,]   •
That such a madcap fellow as thyself
Is entered into our society.
Wife. Ay, but, mylord, he must learn now to put on gravity.
Eyre. Peace, Maggy, a fig for gravity; when I go to
Guildhall in my scarlet gown, I'll look as demurely as a saint,
and speak as gravely as a justice of peace; but now I am
here at Oldford, at my good Lord Mayor's house, let it go by,
vanish, Maggy. I'll be merry; away with flip-flap, these foo-
leries, these gulleries: what, honey? Prince am I none, yet
am I princely born: what says my Lord Mayor?
L. M. Ha, ha, ha! I had rather than a thousand pound, I
had an heart, but half so light as yours.
Eyre. Why, what should I do, mylord? A pound of care
pays not a dram of debt. Hum, let 's be merry, while we
are young; old age, sack and sugar will steal upon us, ere
we be aware.
L. M. It 's well done, Mrs. Eyre: pray, give good counsel
to my daughter.
Wife. I hope, mistress Rose will have the grace, to take
nothing that 's bad.
L. M. Pray God, she do, for i 'faith, Mrs. Eyre,
I would bestow upon that peevish girl
A thousand marks more than I mean to give her,
Upon condition she be ruled by me;
The ape still crosseth me. There came of late
A proper gentleman of fair revenues,
Whom gladly I would call [my] son-in-law:
But my fine cockney would have none of him.
You 'll prove a cockscomb for it, ere you die:
A courtier or no man must please your eye.
Eyre. Be ruled, sweet Rose: thou 'rt ripe for a man;
marry, not with a boy, that has no more hair on his face,
han thou hast on thy cheeks: a courtier, wash go by! Stand
not upon pishery-pashery; those silken fellows are but painted
mages, outsides, outsides, Rose; their inner linings are torn.

No, my fine mouse, marry me with a gentleman-grocer like my Lord Mayor, your father; a grocer is a sweet trade: plums, plums. Had I a son or daughter, should marry out of the generation and blood of the shoemakers, he should pack: what, the gentle trade is a living for a man through Europe, through the world.

A noise within of a tabor and a pipe.

L. M. What noise is this?

Eyre. O my Lord Mayor, a crew of good fellows, that, for love to your honour, are come hither with a morris-dance; come in, my Mesopotamians, cheerily!

Enter Hodge, Hans, Rafe, Firke, and other shoemakers in a morris; after a little dancing the Lord Mayor speaks:

L. M. Master Eyre, are all these shoemakers?

Eyre. All cordwainers, my good Lord Mayor.

Rose. How like my Lacy looks yond shoemaker! [(*Aside.*)]

Hans. O that I durst but speak unto my love! [(*Aside.*)]

L. M. Sibyl, go, fetch some wine to make them drink. You are all welcome.

All.   We thank your Lordship.

Rose takes a cup of wine and goes to Hans.

Rose. For his sake, whose fair shape thou representest Good friend, I drink to thee.

Hans.   Ik bedanke, good frister.

Wife. I see, mistress Rose, you do not want judgment, you have drunk to the properest man I keep.

Firke. Here be some, have done their parts, to be as proper as he.

L. M. Well, urgent business calls me back to London: Good fellows, first go in and taste our cheer, And to make merry, as you homeward go, Spend these two angels in beer at Stratford Bow.

Eyre. To these two, my mad lads, Simon Eyre adds another; then cheerily, Firke; tickle it, Hans; and all for the honour of shoemakers.

(All [shoemakers] go dancing out.)

L. M. Come, master Eyre, let have you company. (*Exeunt*)

Rose. Sibyl, what shall I do?

Sib.   Why, what's the matter?

Rose. That Hans the shoemaker is my love Lacy, Disguised in that attire, to find me out. How should I find the means to speak with him?

Sib. What, mistress, never fear; I dare venter my maidenhead to nothing, and that's great odds, that Hans the Dutchman, when we come to London, shall not only see and speak

with you, but in spite of all your father's policies, steal you
away and marry you. Will not this please you?

Rose. Do this and ever be assured of my love.

Sib. Away then, and follow your father to London, lest
your absence cause him to suspect something.

To morrow, if my counsel be obeyed,
I'll bind you prentice to the gentle trade. [(*Exeunt.*)]

[Scene 12.

London. A Street.]

*Enter Jane in a semster's shop, working, and Hammon,
muffled at another door; he stands aloof.*

Ham. Yonder 's the shop, and there my fair love sits.
She 's fair and lovely, but she is not mine.
O would, she were! Thrice I have courted her,
Thrice hath my hand been moistened with her hand,
Whilst my poor famished eyes do feed on that
Which made them famish. I am infortunate:
I still love one, yet nobody loves me.
I muse, in other men what women see,
That I so want? Fine mistress Rose was coy,
And this too curious! Oh no, she is chaste,
And for she thinks me wanton, she denies,
To cheer my cold heart with her sunny eyes.
How prettily she works! Oh, pretty hand!
Oh happy work! It does me good to stand
Unseen to see her. Thus I oft have stood
In frosty evenings, a light burning by her,
Enduring biting cold, only to eye her.
One only look hath seemed as rich to me,
As a king 's crown; such is lovers' lunacy.
Muffled I'll pass along, and by that try,
Whether she know me.

Jane.　　　　　Sir, what is 't you buy?
What is 't you lack, Sir? — Callico, or lawn,
Fine cambric shirts, or bands, — what will you buy?

Ham. That which thou wilt not sell; faith, yet I 'll try.
　　　　　　　　　　[(*Aside.*)]
How do you sell this handkercher?

Jane.　　　　　Good cheap.

Ham. And how these ruffs?

Jane.　　　　Cheap too.

Ham.　　　　　And how this band?

Jane. Cheap too.

Ham.　　　　All cheap; how sell you then this hand?

Jane. My hands are not to be sold.
Ham. To be given then!
Nay, faith, I come to buy.
Jane. But none knows, when.
Ham. Good sweet, leave work a little while; let 's play.
Jane. I cannot live by keeping holiday.
Ham. I'll pay you for the time, which shall be lost.
Jane. With me you shall not be at so much cost.
Ham. Look, how you wound this cloth, so you wound me.
Jane. It may be so.
Ham. 'T is so.
Jane. What remedy?
Ham. Nay, faith, you are too coy.
Jane. Let go my hand.
Ham. I will do any task at your command,
I would let go this beauty, were I not
In mind, to disobey you by a power
That controlls kings: I love you!
Jane. So, now part.
Ham. With hands I may, but never with my heart.
In faith I love you.
Jane. I believe, you do?
Ham. Shall a true love in me breed hate in you?
Jane. I hate you not.
Ham. Then you must love.
Jane. I do.
What are you better now? I love not you.
Ham. All this, I hope, is but a woman's fray,
That means come to me, when she cries: away!
In earnest mistress, — [for] I do not jest, —
A true chaste love hath entered in my breast;
I love you dearly, as I do my life,
I love you as a husband loves a wife;
That, and no other love, my love requires.
Thy wealth, I know, is little, my desires
Thirst not for gold. Sweet, beauteous Jane, what's mine,
Shall, if thou make my self thine, all be thine.
Say, judge, what is thy sentence, life or death?
Mercy or cruelty lies in thy breath.
Jane. Good sir, I do believe, you love me well:
For 't is a seely conquest, seely pride,
For one like you, — I mean, a gentleman —
To boast, that by his love-tricks he hath brought
Such and such woman to his amorous lure.
I think, yo do not so, yet many do,
And make it even a very trade to woo.
I could be coy, as many women be,

Feed you with sun-shine smiles and wanton looks,
But I detest witch-craft, [and] say, that I
Do constantly believe you, constant have.
Ham. Why doest thou not believe me?
Jane. I believe you.
But yet, good Sir, because I will not grieve you
With hopes to taste fruit, which will never fall:
My husband lives; at least, I hope he lives.
Pressed was he to these bitter wars in France;
Bitter they are to me by wanting him.
I have but one heart, and that heart 's his due.
How can I then bestow the same on you?
Whilst he lives, his I live, be 't ne'er so poor,
And rather be his wife, than a king's whore.
Ham. Chaste and dear woman, I will not abuse thee,
Although it cost my life, if thou refuse me.
Thy husband pressed for France, what was his name?
Jane. Rafe Damport.
                              Damport — here 's a letter sent
From France to me, from a dear friend of mine,
A gentleman of place; here he doth write
Their names, that have been slain in every fight.
Jane. I hope, death's scroll contains not my love's name.
Ham. Can you read?
Jane. [Yes,] I can.
Ham. Peruse the same.
To my remembrance such a name I read
Amongst the rest. See here.
Jane. Ay me, he 's dead!
He 's dead! If this be true, my dear heart 's slain.
Ham. Have patience, dear love.
Jane. Hence, hence!
Ham. Nay, sweet Jane
Make not poor sorrow proud with these rich tears.
I mourn thy husband's death because thou mournest.
Jane. That bill is forged; 't is signed by forgery.
Ham. I'll bring thee letters sent besides to many,
Carrying the like report: Jane, 't is too true.
Come, weep not; mourning, though it rise from love
Helps not the mourned, yet hurts them that mourn.
Jane. For God's sake leave me.
Ham. Whether doest thou turn?
Forget the dead; love them that are alive;
His love is faded; try, how mine will thrive.
Jane. 'T is now no time for me to think on love.
Ham. 'T is now best time for you to think on love,
Because your love lives not.

Jane.   Though he be dead
My love to him shall not be buried.
For God's sake leave me to myself alone.
Ham. 'T would kill my soul, to leave thee drowned in moan.
Answer me to my suit, and I am gone.
Say to me yea or no.
Jane.   No.
Ham.   Then, farewell!
One farewell will not serve, I come again.
Come, dry these wet cheeks; tell me, faith, sweet Jane,
Yea, or no, once more.
Jane.   Once more I say: no!
Once more, begone, I pray, else will I go.
Ham. Nay, then I will grow rude, by this white hand,
Until you change that cold no; here I'll stand,
Till by you, hard heart —
Jane.   Nay, for God's love, peace.
My sorrows by your presence more increase.
Not, that you thus are present, but all grief
Desires to be alone; therefore in brief
Thus much I say, and, saying, bid adieu,
If ever I wed man, it shall be you.
Ham. Oh blessed voice! Dear Jane, I'll urge no more,
Thy breath hath made me rich.
Jane.   Death makes me poor.
                                        (*Exeunt.*)

[Scene 13.

London. The street before Hodge's shop.]

*Enter Hodge at his shop-board, Rafe. Firke, Hans and
a boy at work.*

All. Hey down, a down dery!
Hod. Well said, my hearts; ply your work to day, we
loitered yesterday; to it pell-mell, that we may live to be
Lord Mayors, or aldermen at least.
Firke. Hey down, adown dery!
Hodge. Well said, i 'faith! How sayest thou, Hans? Does
not Firke tickle it?
Hans. Yaw, meester.
Firke. Not so neither; my organ-pipe squeaks this mor-
ning for want of liquoring. Hey down, adown dery!
Hans. Forward, Firke, tow best un jolly youngster. Hort
ye meester, ik bid yo, cut me un pair vamps vor meester
Effre's boots.
Hodge. Thou shalt, Hans.
Firke. Master!

Hodge. How now, boy?

Firke. Pray, now you are in the cutting vein, cut me out a pair of counterfeits, or else my work will not pass current. Hey down, adown!

Hodge. Tell me, sirs, are my cousin Mrs. Priscicall's shoes done?

Firke. Your cousin? No, master, one of your aunts; hang her, let them alone.

Rafe. I am in hand with them: she gave charge, that none but I should do them for her.

Firke. Thou do for her? Then 't will be a lame doing, and that she loves not: Rafe, thou mightst have sent her to me; in faith, I could have yerked and firked your Precilla. Hey down, adown dery! This gear will not hold.

Hodge. How sayest thou, Firke? Where we not merry at Oldford?

Firke. How, merry? why, our buttocks went jiggy-joggy like a quagmire. Well, sir Roger Oatmeal, if I thought all meat of that nature, I would eat nothing but bag-puddings.

Rafe. Of all good fortunes my fellow Hans had the best.

Firke. 'T is true, because mistress Rose drank to him.

Hodge. Well, well, work apace. They say, seven of the aldermen be dead, or very sick.

Firke. I care not, I'll be none.

Rafe. No, nor I; but then Mr. Eyre will come quickly to be Lord Mayor.

Enter Sibyl.

Firke. Whoop, yonder comes Sibyl.

Hodge. Sibyl, welcome, i 'faith; and how doest thou, mad wench?

Firke. Sib-whore, welcome to London.

Sibyl. God-a-mercy, sweet Firke; good Lord, Hodge, what a delicious shop you have got! You tickle it, i 'faith.

Rafe. God-a-mercy, Sibyl, for our good cheer at Oldford.

Sibyl. That you shall have, Rafe.

Firke. Nay, by the mass, we had tickling cheer, Sibyl: and how, the plague, doest thou and mistress Rose, and my Lord Mayor? I put the woman in first.

Sibyl. Well, God-a-mercy: but Gods me, I forget myself; where 's Hans the Fleming?

Firke. Hark, butterbox, now you must yelp out some spreken.

Hans. Vat begaie gon vat vod gon frister?

Sibyl. Marry, you must come to my young mistress, to pull on her shoes, you made last.

Hans. Var been your egle vro? Var been your mistress?

Sibyl. Marry, here at our London house in Cornwall.

Firke. Will nobody serve her turn but Hans?

Sibyl. No, sir. Come, Hans, I stand upon needles.

Hodge. Why then, Sibyl, take heed of pricking.

Sibyl. For that let me alone, I have a trick in my budget.
Come, Hans.

Hans. Yaw, yaw, ik sal meet yo gane.

(Exit Hans and Sibyl.)

Hodge. Go, Hans, make haste again. — Come, who lacks
work?

Firke. I, master, for I lack my breakfast; 't is munching
time, and past.

Hodge. Is 't so? Why, then leave work, Rafe. To breakfast! Boy, look to the tools. Come, Rafe, come Firke.

(Exeunt.)

Enter a serving-man.

Ser. Let me see now the sign of the last in Towerstreet.
Mass! yonder 's the house. What ho! Who's within?

Enter Rafe.

Rafe. Who calls there? What want you, sir?

Ser. Marry, I would have a pair of shoes made for a
gentlewoman against to-morrow morning. What, can you do
them?

Rafe. Yes, Sir, you shall have them. But what length 's
her foot?

Ser. Why, you must make them in all parts like this shoe:
but at any hand fail not to do them, for the gentlewoman
is to be married very early in the morning.

Rafe. How? By this shoe must it be made? By this? Are
you sure sir, by this?

Ser. How, by this am I sure, by this art thou in they
wits? I tell thee, I must have a pair of shoes, doest thou
mark me? A pair of shoes, two shoes, made by this very
shoe, this same shoe, against to-morrow morning by four a
clock. Doest thou understand me? Canst do it?

Rafe. Yes, sir, yes; ay, ay, I can do 't. By this shoe, you
say? I should know this shoe. Yes, sir, yes; by this shoe,
I can do 't; four a clock, well. Whether shall I bring them?

Ser. To the sign of the golden ball in Watlingstreet; in-
quire for one Mr. Hammon, a gentleman, my master.

Rafe. Yea, sir; by this shoe, you say.

Ser. I say, Mr. Hammon at the golden ball; he 's the
bridegroom, and those shoes are for his bride.

Rafe. They shall be done by this shoe; well, well, master
Hammon at the golden shoe, I would say, the golden ball;

well, very well; but I pray you, sir, — where must master
Hammon be married!

Ser. At Saint-Faith's-Church under Paul's. But what 's
that to thee? Prithee, despatch those shoes, and so farewell.

(Exit.)

Rafe. By this shoe, said he. How am I amazed
At this strange accident! Upon my life,
This was the very shoe, I gave my wife,
When I was pressed for France; since when, alas!
I never could hear of her: 't is the same,
And Hammon's bride no other but my Jane.

Enter Firke.

Firke. Snails, Rafe, thou hast lost thy part of three pots,
a countryman of mine gave me to breakfast.

Rafe. I care not; I have found a better thing.

Firke. A thing? Away! Is it a man's thing or a woman's
thing?

Rafe. Firke, doest thou know this shoe?

Firke. No, by my troth; neither doth that know me! I have
no acquaintance with it, 't is a mere stranger to me.

Rafe. Why, then I do. This shoe, I durst be sworn,
Once covered the instep of my Jane.
This is her size, her breadth, thus trod my love;
These true-love knots I pricked; I hold my life,
By this old shoe I shall find out my wife.

Firke. Ha, ha! Old shoe, that were new! How, a murrain,
came this ague-fit of foolishness upon thee?

Rafe. Thus, Firke: even now here came a serving-man;
By this old shoe he 'd have a new pair made,
Against to-morrow morning for his mistress,
That 's to be married to a gentleman.
And why may not this be my sweet[est] Jane?

Firke. And why mayest not thou be my sweet ass? Ha, ha!

Rafe. Well, laugh and spare not, but the truth is this:
Against to-morrow morning I'll provide
A lusty crew of honest shoemakers,
To watch the going of the bride to church:
If she prove Jane, I'll take her, in despite
Of Hammon and the devil, were he by;
If it not be my Jane, what remedy?
Hereof I'm sure, I shall live till I die,
Although I never with a woman lie.

Firke. Thou lie with. a woman, to build nothing but cripple-
gates? Well, God sends fools fortune, and it may be, he light
upon his matrimony by such a device, for wedding and hang-
ing goes by destiny.

[Scene 14.

Loudon.   A room in Sir Roger's house.]

Enter Hans and Rose arm in arm.

Hans.   How happy am I by embracing thee!
O, I did fear such cross mishaps did reign,
That I should never see my Rose again.
Rose.   Sweet Lacy, since fair opportunity
Offers herself to further our escape,
Let not too over-fond esteem of me
Hinder that happy hour.   Invent the means
And Rose will follow thee through all the world.
Hans.   Oh, how I surfeit with excess of joy,
Made happy by thy rich perfection!
But since thou payest sweet interest to my hopes,
Redoubling love on love, let me once more,
Like to a bold-faced debtor crave of thee,
This night to steal abroad; and at Eyre's house,
Who now by death of certain aldermen
Is Mayor of London, and my master once,
Meet thou thy Lacy, where in spite of change,
Your father's anger, and mine uncle's hate
Our happy nuptials will we consummate.

Enter Sibyl.

Sibyl.   Oh God, what will you do, mistress? Shift for your-
self, your father is at hand! He 's coming, he 's coming!
Master Lacy, hide yourself in my mistress! For God's sake,
shift for yourselves.
Hans.   Your father come, sweet Rose — what shall I do?
Where shall I hide me? How shall I escape?
Rose.   A man, and want wit in extremity?
Come, come, be Hans still, play the shoemaker,
Pull on my shoe!

Enter Lord Mayor.

Hans.   Mass! And that's well remembered.
Sibyl.   Here comes your father.
Hans.   Forwar, metresse, 't is un good skow, it fall velout
or ye sall niet betalen.
Rose.   O God, it pincheth me; what will you do?
Hans.   Your father's presence pincheth, not the shoe.
L. M.   Well done; fit my daughter well, and she shall
please thee well.
Hans.   Yaw, yaw, ik weit dat well; forwar 't is un good
skoo; 't is gimait van neit's-leither; se ever, mine her.

Enter a prentice.

L. M. I do believe it. — What 's the news with you?
Prent. Please you, the earl of Lincoln at the gate
Is newly lighted, and would speak with you.
L. M. The earl of Lincoln come [to] speak with me?
Well, well, I know his errand. — Daughter Rose
Send hence your shoemaker, despatch, have done!
Sib, make things handsome! Sir boy, follow me! (*Exit.*)
Hans. My uncle come? O, what may this portend?
Sweet Rose, this of our love threatens an end.
Rose. Be not dismayed at this; what e'er befall,
Rose is thine own. To witness I speak truth,
Where thou appointest the place, I'll meet with thee:
I will not fix a day, to follow thee,
But presently steal hence. Do not reply:
Love which gave strength to bear my father 's hate,
Shall now add wings [to] further our escape. (*Exeunt.*)

[Scene 15.

Another room in the same house.]

Enter Lord Mayor and Lincoln.

L. M. Believe me on my credit, I speak truth:
Since first your nephew Lacy went to France,
I have not seen him. It seemed strange to me,
When Dodger told me, that he stayed behind
Neglecting the high charge the king imposed.
Lin. Trust me, Sir Roger Otley, I did think
Your counsel had given head to this attempt,
Drawn to it by the love he bears your child.
Here I did hope to find him in your house,
But now I see mine error, and confess,
My judgment wronged you by conceiving so.
L. M. Lodge in my house, say you? Trust me, mylord,
I love your nephew Lacy too, too dearly,
So much to wrong his honour; and he hath done so,
That first gave him advice to stay from France.
To witness I speak truth, I let you know,
How careful I have been to keep my daughter
Free from all conference or speech of him.
Not that I scorn your nephew, but in love
I bear your honour, lest your noble blood
Should by my mean worth be dishonoured.
Lin. How far the churl's tongue wanders from his heart.
[(*Aside.*)]
Well, well, sir Roger Otley, I believe you,

4

With more than many thanks for the kind love,
So much you seem to bear me. But, mylord,
Let me request your help to seek my nephew,
Whom if I find, I'll straight embark for France;
So shall your Rose be free, my thoughts at rest,
And much care die, which now lives in my breast.

Enter Sibyl.

Sibyl. Oh Lord! Help for God 's sake! My mistress! Oh my young mistress!

L. M. Where is thy mistress? What 's become of her?

Sibyl. She 's gone, she 's fled!

L. M. Gone! Whither is she fled?

Sibyl. I know not, forsooth; she 's fled out of doors with Hans, the shoemaker, I saw them scud, scud, scud, apace, apace!

L. M. Which way? What, John! Where be my men? Which way?

Sibyl. I know not, an it please your Worship.

L. M. Fled with a shoemaker? Can this be true?

Sibyl. O Lord, sir, as true as God's in heaven.

Lin. Her love turned shoemaker? I'm glad of this.

L. M. A fleming butterbox, a shoemaker!
Will she forget her birth? Requite my care
With such ingratitude? Scorned she young Hammon,
To love an honikin, a needy knave?
Well, let her fly, I'll not fly after her,
Let her starve, if she will; she 's none of mine.

Lin. Be not so cruel, sir.

Enter Firke with shoes.

Sibyl. I'm glad, she 's 'scaped. [(*Aside.*)]

L. M. I'll not accompt of her as of my child,
Was there no better object for her eyes
But a foul drunken lubber swill-belly?
A shoemaker, that 's brave!

Firke. Yea forsooth, 't is a very brave shoe, and as fit as a pudding.

L. M. How now, what knave is this? From whence comest thou?

Firke. No knave, sir. I am Firke the shoemaker, lusty Roger's chief lusty journeyman, and I come hither, to take up the pretty leg of sweet mistress Rose, and thus hoping, your worship is in as good health, as I was at the making hereof, I bid you farewell,

yours,

Firke. [(*Offer to go.*)]

L. M. Stay, stay, sir knave.

Lin. Come hither, shoemaker.

Firke. 'T is happy, the knave is put before the shoemaker, or else I would not have vouchsafed to come back to you. I am moved, for I stir.

L. M. Mylord, this villain calls us knaves by craft.

Firke. Then 't is by the gentle craft, and to call one knave gently, is no harm. Sit your Worship merry. Sib, your young mistress! [(*Aside*)] I'll so bob them, now my master Mr. Eyre is Lord Mayor of London.

L. M. Tell me, sirrah, whose man are you?

Firke. I am glad to see your Worship so merry. I have no maw to this gear, no stomach as yet to a red petticoat.

Lin. He means not, sir, to woo you to this maid, (*Pointing to Sibyl.*) But only doth demand, whose man you are?

Firke. I sing now to the tune of Rogero; Roger, my fellow, is now my master.

Lin. Sirrah, knowest thou one Hans, a shoemaker?

Firke. Hans, shoemaker? oh yes, stay, yes, I have him. I tell you what, I speak it in secret: mistress Rose and he are by this time — no, not so, but shortly are to come to come over one another with „Can you dance the shaking of the sheets?“ It is that Hans, — [(*Aside:*)] I'll so gull these diggers!

L. M. Knowest thou then, where he is?

Firke. Yes, forsooth; yea, marry.

Lin. Canst thou, in sadness —?

Firke. No, forsooth; no, marry.

L. M. Tell me, good honest fellow, where he is, And thou shalt see, what I'll bestow on thee.

Firke. Honest fellow? No, sir; not so, sir: my profession is the gentle craft; I care not for seeing, I love feeling; let me feel it here: *aurium tenus* — ten pieces of gold, *genuum tenus* — ten pieces of silver, and then Firke is your man in a new pair of stretchers.

L. M. Here is an angel, part of thy reward, Which I will give thee; tell me where he is.

Firke. No point! Shall I betray my brother? No! Shall I prove Judas to Hans? No! shall I cry treason to my corporation? No! I shall be firked and yerked then. But give me your angel; your angel shall tell you.

Lin. Do so, good fellow; 't is no hurt to thee.

Firke. Send simpering Sib away.

L. M. Huswife, get you in.

Firke. Pitchers have ears and maids have wide mouths, but for Hans Prance, upon my word, to-morrow morning he and young mistress Rose go to this gear, they shall be married together to this rush, or else turn Firke to a firkin of butter, to tan leather withal.

L. M. But art thou sure of this?

Firke. Am I sure, that Paul's steeple is a handfull higher than London stone? Or that the pissing conduit leaks nothing but pure mother Bunch? Am I sure, I am lusty Firke? Snails, do you think, I am so base, to gull you?

Lin. Where are they married? Doest thou know the church?

Firke. I never go to church, but I know the name of it: it is a swearing church — stay a while, 't is: — Why, by the mass, no! No, it is, by my troth: — No, nor that; 't is, by my faith — that, that 't is, by my Faith's church under Paul's cross. There they shall be knit like a pair of stockings in matrimony; there they 'll be in cony.

Lin. Upon my life, my nephew Lacy walks
In the disguise of this dutch shoemaker.

Firke. Yes, forsooth.

Lin. Doth he not, honest shoemaker?

Firke. No, forsooth, I think, Hans is nobody but Hans, no spirit.

L. M. My mind misgives me now, 't is so indeed.

Lin. My cousin speaks the language, knows the trade.

L. M. Let me request your company, mylord;
Your honourable presence may, no doubt,
Refrain their headstrong rashness, when myself
Going alone, perchance may be o'erborne;
Shall I request this favour?

Lin.   This, or what else.

Firke. Then you must rise betimes, for they mean to fall to their hey passa and repass, pindy-pany, which hand will you have? very early.

L. M. My care shall every way equal their haste;
This night accept your lodging in my house:
The earlier shall we stir, and at Saint Faith's
Prevent this giddy hare-brained nuptial;
This traffick of hot love shall yield cold gains,
They ban our loves and we 'll forbid their banes. *(Exit).*

Lin. At Saint Faith 's Church thou sayest?

Firke.   Yes, by their troth.

Lin. Be secret on thy life.   *(Exit.)*

Firke. Yes, when I kiss your wife! Ha, ha, here 's no craft in the gentle craft. I came hither of purpose with shoes to Sir Roger's worship, whilst Rose his daughter be cony-catched by Hans. Soft now; these two gulls will be at Saint-Faith's church to-morrow morning, to take master bridegroom and mistress bride napping, and they in the meantime shall chop up the matter at the Savoy. But the best sport is, Sir

Roger Otley will find my fellow, lame Rafe's, wife going to
marry a gentleman; and then he 'll stop her instead of his
daughter. O brave, there will be fine tickling sport. Soft now,
what have I to do? O, I know; now a mess of shoemakers
meet at the Woolsack in Ivy-lane, to cozen my gentleman of
lame Rafe's wife', that 's true.

> Alack, alack!
> Girls, hold out tack!
> For now smocks for this jumbling
> Shall go to wrack.   (*Exit.*)

|Scene 16.

A room in Eyre's house.]

Enter Eyre, his wife, Hans and Rose.

Eyre. This is the morning then; stay, my bully, my honest
Hans, is it not?

Hans. This is the morning, that must make us two happy
or miserable. Therefore, if you --

Eyre. Away with these ifs and ands, Hans, and these et
ceteraes. By mine honour, Rowland Lacy, none but the king
shall wrong thee. Come, fear nothing — am I not Sim Eyre?
Is not Sim Eyre Lord Mayor of London? Fear nothing, Rose:
let them all say what they can; dainty, come thou to me —
laughest thou?

Wife. Good mylord, stand her friend in what thing you may.

Eyre. Why, my sweet Lady Madgy, think you Simon Eyre
can forget his fine dutch journeyman? No vah! Fie, I scorn
it, it shall never be cast in my teeth, that I was unthankful.
Lady Madgy, thou hadst never covered thy saracen's-head
with this french flap, nor loaden thy bum with this fardingale,
this trash, trumpery, vanity; Simon Eyre never walked in a
red petticoat, nor wore a chain of gold, but for my fine journeyman's portuguese; and shall I leave him? No! Prince am I
none, yet bear a princely mind.

Hans. Mylord, 't is time for us, to part from hence.

Eyre. Lady Madgy, Lady Madgy, take two or three of my
pie-crust-eaters, my buff-jerkin varlets, that do walk in black
gowns at Simon Eyre's heels; take them, good Lady Madgy;
trip and go, my brown queen of periwigs, with my delicate
Rose and my jolly Rowland to the Savoy: see them linked,
countenance the marriage; and when it is done, cling, cling
together, you Hambrough turtle-doves: I'll bear you out; come
to Simon Eyre, come dwell with me, Hans; thou shalt eat
minced-pies and marchpane. Rose, away, cricket; trip and go,
mylady Madgy, to the Savoy; Hans, wed and to bed, kiss and
away; go, vanish!

Wife. Farewell, mylord.

Rose. Make haste, sweet love.

Wife.   She 'd fain, the deed were done.

Hans. Come, my sweet Rose, faster than deer we'll run.

            ([*Mrs. Eyre, Hans and Rose*] *exeunt.*)

Eyre. Go, vanish, vanish! Avaunt, I say! — By the Lord of Ludgate, 't is a mad life to be a Lord Mayor; 't is a stirring life, a fine life, a velvet life, a careful life. Well, Simon Eyre, yet set a good face on it, in the honour of Saint Hugh. — Soft, the king this day comes to dine with me, to see my new buildings. His majesty is welcome: he shall have good cheer, delicate cheer, princely cheer. This day my fellow prentices of London come to dine with me, too: they shall have fine cheer, gentleman-like cheer. I promised the mad Cappadosians, when we all served at the Conduit together, that if ever I came to be Mayor of London, I would feast them all, and I'll do 't. I'll do 't by the life of Pharaoh; by this beard, Sim Eyre will be no flincher. Besides, I have procured, that upon every Shrove-tuesday, at the sound of the pancake-bell, my fine dapper Assyrian lads shall clap up their shop-windows, and away. This is the day, and this day they shall do 't, they shall do 't.

    Boys, that day are you free, let masters care,
    And prentices shall pray for Simon Eyre.   *(Exit.)*

[Scene 17.

A street near Saint Faith's church.]

Enter Hodge, Firke, Rose, and six or five shoemakers, all with cudgels or such weapons.

Hodge. Come, Rafe; stand to it, Firke. My masters, as we are the brave bloods of the shoemakers, heirs apparent to Saint Hugh, and perpetual benefactors to all good fellows, thou shalt have no wrong; were Hammon a king of spades, he should not delve in thy close without thy sufferance; but tell me, Rafe: art thou sure, 't is thy wife?

Rafe. Am I sure, this is Firke? This morning, when I stroked on her shoes, I looked upon her, and she upon me, and sighed and asked me, if ever I knew one Rafe. Yes, said I. „For his sake,“ said she, tears standing in here yes, „and for thou art somewhat like him, spend this piece of gold.“ I took it; my lame leg and my travel beyond sea made me unknown. All is one for that: I know, she's mine.

Firke. Did she give thee this gold? O glorious, glittering gold! She 's thine own, 't is thy wife, and she loves thee, for I'll stand to 't, there 's no woman will give gold to any man, but she thinks better of him, than she thinks of them, she gives silver to. And for Hammon, neither Hammon nor hangman shall wrong thee in London. Is not our old master Eyre Lord Mayor? Speak, my hearts.

All. Yes, and Hammon shall know it to his cost.

Enter Hammon, his man, and Jane, and others.

Hodge. Peace, my bullies, yonder they come.

Rafe. Stand to 't, my hearts. Firke, let me speak first.

Hodge. No, Rafe; let me. Hammon, whither away so early?

Ham. Unmannerly rude slave, what's that to thee?

Firke. To him, sir? Yes, sir; and to me, and others. Good morrow, Jane, how doest thou? Good Lord, how the world is changed with you! God be thanked!

Ham. Villains, hands off! How dare you touch my love?

All. Villains? Down with them! Cry clubs for prentices.

Hodge. Hold, my hearts! Touch her, Hammon? Yea, and more than that: we 'll carry her away with us. My masters and gentlemen, never draw your bird-spits; shoemakers are steel to the back, men every inch of them, all spirit.

All of Hammon's side. Well, and what of all this?

Hodge. I'll shew you: Jane, doest thou know this man? 'T is Rafe, I can tell thee; nay, 't is he in faith, though he be lamed by the wars. Yet look not strange, but run to him, fold him about the neck and kiss him.

Jane. Lives then my husband? Oh God, let me go,
Let me embrace my Rafe.

Ham.   What means my Jane?

Jane. Nay, what meant you, to tell me, he was slain?

Ham. [O] pardon me, dear love; for, being missed,
'T was rumoured here in London, thou wert dead.

[(*To Rafe.*)]

Firke. Thou seest, he lives. Lass, go pack home with him. Now, Mr. Hammon, where's your mistress? your wife?

Serv. 'Swounds, master, fight for her! Will you thus lose her?

All. Down with that creature! Clubs! Down with him!

Hodge. Hold! Hold!

Ham.   Hold, fool! Sirs, he shall do no wrong.
Will my Jane leave me thus and break her faith?

Firke. Yes, sir! She must, sir! She shall, sir! What then? Mend it!

Hodge. Hark, fellow Rafe, follow my counsel: set the wench in the midst, and let her choose her man, and let her be his woman.

Jane. Whom should I choose? Whom should my thoughts
                                        affect,

But him, whom heaven hath made to be my love?
Thou art my husband, and these humble weeds
Makes thee more beautiful than all his wealth.
Therefore I will but put off his attire,
Returning it into the owner's hand,
And after ever be thy constant wife.

Hodge. Not a rag, Jane! The law 's on our side. He that sows in another man 's ground, forfeits his harvest. Get thee home, Rafe; follow him, Jane; he shall not have so much as a busk-point from thee.

Firke. Stand to that, Rafe, the appurtenances are thine own. Hammon, look not at her.

Serv. O, 'swounds, no!

Firke. Blue-coat, be quiet; we 'll give you a new livery else, we 'll make Shrove-tuesday Saint-Georges' day for you. Look not, Hammon, leer not! I'll firk you! For thy head now, one glance, one sheep's-eye, anything at her. Touch not a rag, lest I and my brethren beat you to clouts.

Serv. Come, master Hammon, there 's no striving here.

Ham. Good fellows, hear me speak; and, honest Rafe,
Whom I injured most by loving Jane,
Mark what I offer thee: here in fair gold
Is twenty pound, I'll give thee for thy Jane;
If this content thee not, thou shalt have more.

Hodge. Sell not thy wife, Rafe; make her not a whore.

Ham. Say, wilt thou freely cease thy claim in her,
And let her be my wife?

All.   No, do not, Rafe.

Rafe. Sirrah Hammon, doest thou think, a shoemaker is so base, to be a bawd to his own wife for commodity? Take thy gold, choke with it! Were I not lame, I would make thee eat thy words.

Firke. A shoemaker sell his flesh and blood? Oh, indignity!

Hodge. Sirrah, take up yourself, and be packing.

Ham. I will not touch one penny, but in lieu
Of that great wrong, I offered thy Jane,
To Jane and thee I give that twenty pound.
Since I have failed of her, during my life,
I vow, no woman else shall be my wife.
Farewell, good fellows of the gentle trade.
Your morning mirth my mourning day hath made. *(Exit.)*

Firke. Touch the gold, creature, if you dare! Y'are best be trudging. Here, Jane, take thou it. Now let 's home, my hearts.

Hodge. Stay, who comes here? Jane, on again with thy mask!

Enter Lincoln, Lord Mayor, and servants.

Lin. Yonder 's the lying varlet mocked us so.
L. M. Come hither, sirrah!
Firke. I, sir? I am sirrah? You mean me, do you not?
Lin. Where is my nephew married?
Firke. Is he married? God give him joy, I am glad of it;
They have a fine day, and the sign is in a good planet, Mars
in Venus.
L. M. Villain, thou toldst me, that my daughter Rose
This morning should be married at Saint Faith's.
We have watch there these three hours at the least,
Yet see we no such thing.
Firke. Truly, I am sorry for it; a bride is a pretty thing.
Hodge. Come to the purpose. Yonder 's the bride and
bridegrom, you look for, I hope. Though you be lords, you
are not to bar by your authority men from women. Are you?
L. M. See, see, my daughter 's masked.
Lin.   True, and my nephew
To hide his guilt [now], counterfeits him lame.
Firke. Yea truly, God help the poor couple, they are lame
and blind.
L. M. I'll ease her blindness.
Lin.   I'll his lameness cure.
Firke. Lie down, sirs, and laugh! My fellow Rafe is taken
for Rowland Lacy, and Jane for mistress damask-Rose. This
is all my knavery.
L. M. What, have I found you, minion?
Lin.   O base wretch!
Nay, hide thy face, the horror of thy guilt
Can hardly be washed off. Where are thy powers?
What battles have you made? O yes, I see,
Thou foughtst with shame and shame hath conquered thee.
This lameness will not serve.
L. M.   Unmask yourself!
Lin. Lead home your daughter.
L. M.   Take your nephew hence.
Rafe. Hence? 'Swounds, what ween you? Are you mad?
I hope, you cannot enforce my wife from me. Where 's
Hammon?
L. M. Your wife?
Lin. What Hammon?
Rafe. Yea, my wife; and therefore the proudest of you,
that lays hand on her first, I'll lay my crutch cross his pate.
Firke. To him, lame Rafe! Here's brave sport!
Rafe. Rose call you her? Why her name is Jane. Look
here else; do you know her now?   [(*Unmasking Jane.*)]

5

Lin. Is this your daughter?

L. M.   No, nor this your nephew.
Mylord of Lincoln, we are both abused
By this base, crafty varlet.

Firke. Yea forsooth, no varlet; forsooth, no base; forsooth,
I am but mean; not crafty neither, but of the gentle craft.

L. M. Where is my daughter Rose? Where is my child?

Lin. Where is my nephew Lacy married?

Firke. Why, here is good laced mutton, as I promised you.

Lin. Villain, I'll have thee punished for this wrong.

Firke. Punish the journeyman villain, but not the journeyman shoemaker.

Enter Dodger.

Dodg. Mylord, I come to bring unwelcome news.
Your nephew Lacy, and your daughter Rose
Early this morning wedded at the Savoy,
None being present but the Lady Mayoress.
Besides I learned among the officers,
The Lord Mayor vows, to stand in their defence,
'Gainst any that shall seek to cross the match.

Lin. Dares Eyre the shoemaker uphold the deed?

Firke. Yes, sir, shoemakers dare stand in a woman's
quarrel, I warrant, as deep as another, and deeper too.

Dodg. Besides, his Grace to-day dines with the mayor,
Who on his knees humbly intends to fall,
And beg a pardon for your nephew's fault.

Lin. But I'll prevent him. Come, sir Roger Otley;
The king will do us justice in this cause.
How! Ere their hands have made them man and wife,
I will disjoin the match, or lose my life.

        (*Exeunt* [*L. Mayor, Lincoln and Dodger.*])

Firke. Adieu, mounsieur Dodger! Farewell, fools! Ha! Ha!
Oh, if they had stayed, I would have so lambed them with
flouts. O heart, my codpeece-point is ready to fly in pieces
every time I think upon mistress Rose; but let that pass, as
mylady Mayoress says.

Hodge. This matter is answered. Come, Rafe; home with
thy wife; come, my fine shoemakers, let's to our master's,
the new Lord Mayor, and there swagger this Shrove-tuesday;
I'll promise you wine enough, for Madge keeps the cellar.

All. O rare! Madge is a good wench.

Firke. And I'll promise you meat enough, for simpering
Susan keeps the larder. I'll lead you to victuals, my brave
soldiers; follow your captain. O brave! Hark, hark!

                              (*Bell rings.*)

All. The pancake-bell rings, the pancake-bell! Tri-lill,
my hearts!

Firke. O brave! O sweet bell! O delicate pancakes! Open the door, my hearts, and shut up the windows. Keep in the house, let out the pancakes! Oh rare, my hearts! Let 's march together for the honour of Saint Hugh, to the great new hall in Gracious-street corner, which our master, the new Lord Mayor, hath built.

Rafe. O the crew of good fellows, that will dine at mylord Mayor's cost to-day.

Hodge. The Lord Mayor is a most brave man. How shall prentices be bound to pray for him and the honour of the gentlemen shoemakers! Let's feed and be fat with mylord Mayor's bounty.

Firke. O musical bell still! O Hodge, o my brethren, there 's cheer for the heavens, venison-pasties walk up and down piping-hot, like sergeants; beef and brewis comes marching in dry-fats, fritters and pancakes come trolling in wheel-barrows, hens and oranges hopping in porter's-baskets, collops and eggs in scuttles, and tarts and custards comes quavering in malt-shovels.

Enter more prentices.

All. Whoop, look here!

Hodge. How now, mad lads? Whither away so fast?

1. Prent. Whither? Why, to the great new hall, know you not why? The Lord Mayor hath bidden all the prentices in London to breakfast this morning.

All. Oh brave shoemaker, oh brave Lord of incomprehensible good fellowship! Who! Hark you? The pancake-bell rings.
(Cast up caps.)

Firke. Nay, more, my hearts: every Shrove-tuesday is our year of jubilee; and when then pancake-bell rings, we are as free as my Lord Mayor; we may shut up our shops and make holiday: I'll have it called Saint Hugh's holiday.

All. Agreed, agreed, Saint Hugh's holiday.

Hodge. And this shall continue for ever.

All. Oh brave! Come, come, my hearts! Away, away!

Firke. O eternal credit to us of the gentle craft! March fair, my hearts! O rare!   *(Exeunt.)*

[Scene 18.

London. A street.]

Enter the king, and his train over the stage.

King. Is our Lord Mayor of London such a gallant?

Nobleman. One of the merriest madcaps in your land. Your Grace will think, when you behold the man,

He 's rather a wild ruffian, than a Mayor.
Yet thus much I'll ensure your Majesty,
In all his actions, that concern his state,
He is as serious, provident and wise,
As full of gravity among the grave,
As any Mayor hath been these many years.
King. I am with child, till I behold this huff-cap,
But all my doubt is, when we come in presence,
His madness will be dashed clean out of countenance.
Nobl. It may be so, my liege.
King.   Which to prevent,
Let some one give him notice, 't is our pleasure,
That he put on his wonted merriment.
Set forward!
All.   On afore!   *(Exeunt.)*

[Scene 19.

A great hall.]

*Enter Eyre, Hodge, Firke, Rafe, and other shoemakers,
all with napkins on their shoulders.*

Eyre. Come, my fine Hodge, my jolly gentlemen shoemakers; soft, where be these cannibals, these varlets, my officers?
Let them all walk and wait upon my brethren, for my meaning
is, that none but shoemakers, none but the livery of my company shall in their satin hoods wait upon the trencher of my
sovereign.

Firke. O mylord, it will be rare.

Eyre. No more, Firke, come lively, let your fellow prentices want no cheer; let wine be plentiful as beer, and beer
as water. Hang these penny-pinching fathers, that cram wealth
in innocent lamb's skins. Rip, knaves! Avaunt! Look to my
guests.

Hodge. Mylord, we are at our wit's end for room: those
hundred tables will not feast the fourth part of them.

Eyre. Then cover me those hundred tables again and again,
till all my jolly prentices have feasted. Avoid, Hodge! Run,
Rafe! Frisk about, my nimbly Firke! Carouse me fadom-deep
healths to the honour of shoemakers. Do they drink lively,
Hodge? Do they tickle it, Firke?

Firke. Tickle it? Some of them have taken their liquor
standing so long, that they can stand no longer. But for meat,
they would eat it, an they had it.

Eyre. Want they meat? Where 's this swag-belly, this
greasy kitchin-stuff cook? Call the varlet to me! Want meat?
Firke, Hodge, lame Rafe, run up, my tall men, beleaguer the

shambles, beggar all Eastcheap, serve me whole oxen in chargers! And let sheep whine upon the table like pigs, for want of good fellows to eat them. Want meat? Vanish Firke! Avaunt, Hodge!

Hodge. Your Lordship mistakes my man Firke; he means, their bellies want meat, not the boards, for they have drunk so much, they can eat nothing.

Enter Hans, Rose and Wife.

Wife. Where is mylord?

Eyre. How now, Lady Madgy?

Wife. The king's most excellent Majesty is new come. He sends me for thy Honour; one of his most worshipful peers bad me tell, thou must be merry and so forth; but let that pass.

Eyre. Is my sovereign come! Vanish, my tall shoemakers! My nimble brethren, look to my guests, the prentices. Yet stay a little: how now, Hans? How looks my little Rose?

Hans. Let me request you to remember me. I know, your Honour easily may obtain Free pardon of the king for me and Rose, And reconcile me to my uncle's grace.

Eyre. Have done, my good Hans, my honest journeyman; look cheerily; I'll fall upon both my knees, till they be as hard as horn, but I'll get thy pardon.

Wife. Good mylord, have a care, what you speak to his Grace.

Eyre. Away, you Islington whitepot! Hence, you hopper-arse! You barley-pudding, full of maggots! You broiled carbonado! Avaunt, avaunt, avoid, Mephistophilus! Shall Simon Eyre learn to speak of you, Lady Madgy? Vanish, mother minever-cap; vanish, go, trip and go; meddle with your platters and your pishery-pashery, your flews and your whirligigs; go, rub out of mine alley! Sim Eyre knows how to speak to a pope, to sultan Soliman, to Tamberlain, an he were here; and shall I melt, shall I droop before my sovereign? No, come, mylady Madgy! Follow me, Hans! About your business, my frolick freebooters! Firke, frisk about, and about, and about, for the honour of mad Simon Eyre, Lord Mayor of London.

Firke. Hey for the honour of shoemakers! *(Exeunt.)*

[Scene 20.

An open yard before the hall.]

A long flourish or two. Enter the king, nobles, Eyre, his wife, Lacy, Rose. Lacy and Rose kneel.

King. Well, Lacy, though the fact was very foul Of your revolting from our kingly love

And your own duty, yet we pardon you.
Rise both, and, Mrs. Lacy, thank my Lord Mayor
For your young bridegroom here.

Eyre. So, my deer liege, Sim Eyre and my brethren, the
gentlemen shoemakers, shall set your sweet Majesty's image
cheek by jole by Saint Hugh, for this honour you have done
poor Simon Eyre. I beseech your Grace, pardon my rude
behaviour; I am a handicraft's-man, yet my heart is without
craft. I should be sorry at my soul, that my boldness should
offend my king.

King. Nay, I pray thee, good Lord Mayor, be even as merry
As if thou wert among thy shoemakers;
It does me good to see thee in this humour.

Eyre. Sayest thou so, my sweet Dioclesian? Then, hump!
Prince am I none, yet am I princely born. By the Lord of
Ludgate, my liege, I'll be as merry as a pie.

King. Tell me in faith, mad Eyre, how old thou art.

Eyre. My liege, a very boy, a stripling, a yonker; you see
not a white hair on my head, not a gray in this beard. Every
hair, I assure thy Majesty, that sticks in this beard, Sim Eyre
values at the king of Babylon's ransom. T..mar Cham's beard
was a rubbing brush to 't; yet I'll shave it off and stuff ten-
nis-balls with it, to please my bully king.

King. But all this while I do not know your age.

Eyre. My liege, I am six and fifty years old, yet I can
cry, hump! with a sound heart, for the honour of Saint Hugh.
Mark this old wench, my king: I danced the shaking of the
sheet with her six and thirty years ago, and yet I hope to
get two or three Lord Mayors, ere I die; I am lusty still,
Sim Eyre still; care and cold lodging brings white hairs. My
sweet Majesty, let care vanish; cast it upon the nobles; it will
make thee look always young like Apollo; and cry hump!
Prince am I none, yet am I princely born.

King. Ha, ha!
Say, Cornwall, didst thou ever see his like?

Nobl. Not I, mylord.

Enter Lincoln and Lord Mayor.

King. Lincoln, what news with you?

Lin. My gracious Lord, have care unto yourself,
For there are traitors here.

All. Traitors? Where? Who?

Eyre. Traitors in my house? God forbid! Where be my officers?
I'll spend my soul, ere my king feel harm.

King. Where is the traitor, Lincoln?

Lin. Here he stands.

King. Cornwall, lay hands on Lacy! Lincoln, speak,
What canst thou lay unto thy nephew's charge?

Lin. This, my dear liege: your Grace, to do me honour,
Heaped on the head of this degenerous boy
Desertless favours; you made choice of him,
To be commander over powers in France;
But he —
King. Good Lincoln, prithee, pause a while.
Even in thy eyes I read what thou wouldst speak.
I know, how Lacy did neglect our love,
Ran himself deeply, in the highest degree,
Into vile treason.
Lin. Is he not a traitor?
King. Lincoln, he was; now have we pardoned him
'T was not a base want of true valour's fire,
That held him out of France, but love's desire.
Lin. I will not bear his shame upon my back.
King. Nor shalt thou, Lincoln, I forgive you both.
Lin. Then, good my liege, forbid the boy to wed
One whose mean birth will much disgrace his bed.
King. Are they not married?
Lin. No, my liege.
Both. We are.
King. Shall I divorce them then? O, be it far,
That any hand on earth should dare untie
The sacred knot, knit by God's majesty;
I would not for my crown disjoin their hands,
That are conjoined in holy nuptial bands.
How sayest thou, Lacy? Wouldst thou loose thy Rose?
Hans. Not for all Indian's wealth, my sovereign.
King. But Rose, I'm sure, her Lacy would forego.
Rose. If Rose were asked that question, she 'd say no.
King. You hear then, Lincoln.
Lin. Yea, my liege, I do.
King. And canst thou find in heart, to part these two? —
Who seeks besides you to divorce these lovers?
L. M. I do, my gracious lord; I am her father.
King. Sir Roger Otley, our last Mayor, I think?
Nobl. The same, my liege.
King. Would you offend Love's laws?
Well, you shall have your wills; you sued to me,
To prohibite the match: Soft let me see —
You both are married, Lacy, art thou not?
Hans. I am, dread sovereign.
King. Then, upon thy life,
I charge thee, not to call this woman wife.
L. M. I thank your Grace.
Rose. O my most gracious Lord! *(kneel.)*
King. Nay, Rose, never woo me; I tell you true,

Although as yet I am a bachelor,
Yet I believe, I shall not marry you.
Rose. Can you divide the body from the soul,
Yet make the body live?
King. Yea, so profound?
I cannot, Rose; but you I must divide.
This fair maid, bridegroom, cannot be your bride.
Are you pleased, Lincoln? Otley, are you pleased!
Both. Yes, mylord [,yes].
King. Then must my heart be eased.
For credit me, my conscience lives in pain,
Till these, whom I divorced, be joined again.
Lacy, give me thy hand; Rose, lend me thine —
Be what you would be! Kiss now! So, that's fine.
At night, lovers, to bed! Now let me see,
Which of you all mislikes this harmony?
L. M. Will you then take from me my child perforce?
King. Why, tell me, Otley: shines not Lacy's name
As bright in the world 's eye, as the gay beams
Of any citizen?
Lin. Yea, but, my gracious lord,
I do mislike the match far more than he;
Her blood is too, too base.
King. Lincoln, no more.
Doest thou not know, that love respects no blood?
Cares not for difference of birth or state?
The maid is young, well-born, fair, virtuous,
A worthy bride for any gentleman.
Besides, your nephew for her sake did stoop
To bare necessity; aud, as I hear,
Forgetting honours and all courtly pleasures,
To gayie her love, became a shoemaker.
As for the honour, which he lost in France,
Thus I redeem it: Lacy, kneel thee down! —
Arise, Sir Rowland Lacy! Tell me now,
Tell me in earnest, Otley, canst thou chide,
Seeing thy Rose a lady and a bride?
L. M. I am content with what your Grace hath done.
Lin. And I, my liege, since there's no remedy.
King. Come on then, all shake hands: I'll have you friends.
Where there is [so] much love, all discord ends.
What says my mad Lord Mayor to all this love?
Eyre. O my liege, this honour you have done to my fine
journeyman here, Rowland Lacy, and all these favour[s], which
you have shown to me this day in my poor house, will make
Simon Eyre live longer by one dozen of warm summers more
than he should.

King. Nay, my mad Lord Mayor, (that shall be thy name,)
If any grace of mine can length thy life,
One honour more I'll do thee: that new building,
Which at thy cost in Cornhill is erected,
Shall take a name from us; we'll have it called
The Leadenhall, because in digging it
You found the lead, that covereth the same.
Eyre. I thank your Majesty.
Wife.   God bless your Grace.
King. Lincoln, a word with you.

Enter Hodge, Firke, and more shoemakers.

Eyre. How now, my mad knaves? Peace, speak softly,
yonder is the king.
King. With the old troop, which there we keep in pay,
We will incorporate a new supply.
Before one summer more pass o'er my head,
France shall repent, England was injured. —
What are those?
Hans.   All shoemakers, my liege.
Sometimes my fellows; in their companies
I lived as merry as an emperor.
King. My mad Lord Mayor, are all these shoemakers?
Eyre. All shoemakers, my liege; all gentlemen of the gentle
craft, true Trojans, courageous cordwainers; they all kneel to
the shrine of holy Saint Hugh.
All. God save your Majesty.
King. Mad Simon, would they anything with us?
Eyre. Mum, mad knaves! Not a word! I'll do 't, I war-
rant you. They are all beggars, my liege; all for themselves
and I for them all, on both my knees do entreat, that for th[e
ho]nour of poor Simon Eyre, and the good of his brethren,
[these] mad knaves, your Grace would vouchsafe some privi-
lege to my new Leadenhall, that it may be lawful for us, to
buy and sell leather there two days in a week.
King. Mad Sim, I grant your suit, you shall have patent,
To hold two market-days in Leadenhall
Mondays and Fridays, those shall be the times.
Will this content you?
All.   Jesus bless your Grace!
Eyre. In the name of these my poor brethren shoemakers,
I most humbly thank your Grace. But before I rise, seeing,
you are in the giving vein, and we in the begging, grant Sim
Eyre one boon more.
King. What is it, my Lord Mayor?
Eyre. Vouchsafe to taste of our banquet, that 's sweetly
waiting for your sweet presence.

King. I shall undo thee, Eyre, only with this.
Already have I been to troublesome;
Say, have I not?
Eyre. O my dear king, Sim Eyre cannot think so.   Upon
a shroving, which I promised to all the merry prentices of
London — for, an 't please you, when I was prentice,
   I bare the water-tankard, and my coat
Sits not a whit the worse upon my back;
And then, upon a morning, some mad boys,
('T was Shrove-tuesday, even as 't is now,)
Gave me my breakfast, and [I swo]re then b[y] the st . . .
my tankard, if ever I [should become Mayor of London, I]
would feast the prentices . . . .
the slaves had an hundred t . . . .
gone home and vanished . . . .
   Yet add more glory to . . . .
   Taste of Eyre's banquet   . . . .
King. I will taste of thy banquet, [and wi]ll say,
I have not met more pleasure on a day.
Friends of the gentle craft, thanks to you all!
Thanks my kind Lady Mayoress for our cheer:
C . . . . us a while, let's revel it at home.
[When a]ll our words and banquetings are done,
We must right wrongs, which Frenchmen have begun.

                                  [(*Exeunt.*)]

` F i n i s.

Bemerkungen.

Der in den „Jahrbüchern für romanische und englische Literatur" Band II. p. 455 ausgesprochene Wunsch, dass „The Shoemaker's Holiday" neu herausgegeben werden möchte, ist hiemit erfüllt, so gut es das Original, welches mir zu Gebote stand, und meine Kraft erlaubten. Der alte Druck, eine Quartausgabe von 65 Seiten, meistens Blackletterdruck, befindet sich, mit mehreren gleichzeitigen, schon bekannten Schauspielen und andern Schriftwerken zusammengebunden, auf der Danziger Stadtbibliothek. Obwohl der Band sonst wohl erhalten ist, hat doch grade dieses Stück einige durch Wurmfrass und sonstige Verstümmlungen entstandene Lücken; das letzte Blatt ist so zerrissen, dass ich nur zum kleinsten Theile das Fehlende zu ergänzen wagen konnte. Doch würde dies anderweit möglich sein, da sich meine Vermuthung, die ich, auf vergebliches Suchen in Catalogen und Sammelwerken gestützt, im „Archiv für Studium der neueren Sprachen und Literaturen" Band XXVI. p. 81 aussprach, dass nämlich das Danziger Exemplar vielleicht das einzig erhaltene wäre, sich nicht als richtig erwiesen hat. In dem früher vergeblich durchsuchten Glossar von Nares fanden sich schliesslich mehrere Citate, welche beweisen, dass von dem Stücke ein noch früherer Druck, aus dem Iahre 1610, existirt, welcher Nares und Steevens bekannt war,*) so dass also in England jedenfalls noch ein, wohl auch mehrere Exemplare unseres Lustspiels vorhanden sind. Nichtsdestoweniger wird seine Herausgabe den Freunden des altenglischen Theaters

---

*) Siehe Nares, (Stralsunder Ausgabe) s. v. Scant, p. 701, zu Sc. 2, p. 12; Threeman's song, p. 807, zu den vorgedruckten Liedern; Od's pitikins, p. 551, zu Sc. 6, p. 19, wo aber God's pitikins in der Ausgabe von 1618 steht; Go by, Jeronimo, p. 325, zu Sc. 2, p. 12; castilian liquor, p. 110, zu Sc. 4, p. 16.

immerhin noch willkommen sein, da das bis jetzt vergessene Stück manche interessante Seite bietet: die Schilderung des Londoner Handwerkerlebens in jener Zeit, das Auftreten plattdeutsch redender Personen, die an historische Vorgänge sich anlehnende Fabel.

„The shoemaker's holiday" oder „the gentle craft" — womit wie in Robert Green's „Pinner of Wakefield" das Schuhmacherhandwerk gemeint ist — erweist sich als ein Volksstück, auf den Geschmack von Lehrlingen, Gesellen und Spiessbürgern berechnet. Es fehlt darin nicht an Trommeln und Pfeifen, einem Aufzuge, Tanz und Maskerade, nationalen Prahlereien, Rührscenen und Zoten. Die Verherrlichung der Zunft ist Hauptzweck des wie auf Bestellung zu einem Feste gearbeiteten Stücks. Schustergesellen sind die Hauptpersonen, ein Schuhmachermeister kommt zu Geld und Ehre, und bewirthet sogar den König. Nur bemerkt man leider nicht das Verdienst des tollen Meisters; er wird Sheriff und Lord Mayor, ohne dass man recht sieht, dass er dieser Auszeichnungen würdig ist; und dass er Vermögen erwirbt, ist nur ein Zufall, nicht sein Verdienst, da sogar sein Gesell, ein als Schuhmacher verkleideter Edelmann, ihn auf die Gelegenheit aufmerksam machen und ihm Geld vorschiessen muss. Dennoch ist die Lebendigkeit des Dialogs, der unterhaltende Wechsel der Scenen nicht ohne Interesse, und gut gespielt wird das Stück schon in seinem Kreise Beifall errungen haben. Dafür spricht schon der Umstand, dass es zwei Auflagen erlebte, 1610 und 1618, und dass, vorausgesetzt, die weiter unten folgende Bestimmung seiner Entstehungszeit sei richtig, es sich etwa 20 Jahre lang so gut in dem Gedächtnisse des Publicums gehalten hat, um noch eine Wiederholung des Druckes im Jahre 1618 wünschenswerth erscheinen zu lassen.*) Vielleicht enthält Rowley's „Shoemaker a gentleman", ein Stück, welches ich nicht kenne, (gedruckt 1638) eine ähnliche Geschichte. Wie in den meisten Stücken der Zeit ist auch hier die übliche Verknüpfung von zwei, selbst drei Fabeln eine ziemlich lose, obgleich der Verfasser, dem es an Bühnenkenntniss offenbar nicht gefehlt hat, bei geringerer Flüchtigkeit sein Gewebe oft durch Einschlag weniger Fäden in einen festeren Zusammenhang hätte bringen können. Wie Lacy hoffen kann, durch seine Verkleidung als Schuhmacher und seine Arbeit bei Eyre sich Rosen zu nähern, ist nicht einmal ausgesprochen, so nahe

---

*) Die Ausgaben können nicht ganz gleich sein, denn abgesehen davon dass die Seitenzahl der Citate bei Nares mit der Ausgabe von 1618, welche mir vorliegt, nicht stimmt, heist es bei Nares p. 551 Od's pitikins, wo die 2. Ausgabe God's pitikins hat, ein keineswegs bedeutungsloser Unterschied.

es auch lag. Am besten ist noch die Geschichte Rafe's, Jane's und Hammon's in die Abenteuer Eyre's und Lacy's (dessen Reden ich nach dem Original von dem Schluss der 7. Scene an mit „Hans" bezeichne,) eingeflochten. — Andrerseits ist Manches überflüssig angebracht, ohne allen wesentlichen Zweck; dass Lacy sich als Schuhmacher verkleidet, mag hingehen, aber wozu als deutscher Schuhmacher, der sein Gewerbe in Wittenberg, wie Hamlet Philosophie, getrieben hat? Ein englischer Gesell hätte dieselben Dienste gethan, aber die Nachahmung einer fremden Sprache gab Gelegenheit zu lustigen Einfällen und Gelächter, und das war der Zweck des Dichters. — Die Charactere sind nicht ohne Geschick gezeichnet, der Gegensatz des bürgerlich hochmüthigen Otley und des adlich hochmüthigen Lincoln sogar recht gut hervorgehoben; nur die Persönlichkeit Hammon's ist ganz verfehlt und ohne allen Halt. Interessant ist es, dass die Fabel, soweit sie Eyre's Erhebung zur Lordmayor'swürde und die Erbauung Leadenhall's betrifft, einen historischen Anhalt hat. In einem Handbuch über London (Leigh's New Pictures of London; London 1834) fand ich p. 9: „In this reign (Heinrich des fünften) Sir Thomas Eyre, mayor, built Leadenhall for a public granary." Zwar heisst dieser Eyre Thomas und der Held unseres Stückes Simon, indessen sollte wohl durch den Namen Simon, welcher etwa die Nebenbedeutung hat, die sich bei uns mit Hans, Peter, Michel und ähnlichen verknüpft, die lustige Verschrobenheit des Benannten angedeutet werden. Auch das „Sir" lässt sich erklären; daraus, dass die Mayors von London, die, wie Eyre, vom Könige in der Guildhall einen Besuch erhalten, in den Baronetsrang erhoben zu werden pflegen. — Leadenhall-market ist heutzutage „the greatest in London for the sale of country-killed meat and was, till lately, the only skin and leather-market within the bills of mortality" (Leigh, p. 108.) *) Ist es richtig, dass Sir Thomas Eyre Leadenhall zum Kornspeicher erbaute, so verliert dadurch freilich die Annahme, dass der König des Stückes Heinrich V, Simon Eyre den Sir Thomas Eyre vorstellen soll, ein Geringes an Glaublichkeit; doch beweist der Schluss des Stückes, der unserm Simon die Erbauung von Leadenhall, wenn auch zu einem andern Zwecke, als um als Kornspeicher zu dienen, beimisst, immer wenigstens so viel, dass eine Vermischung historischer Facta mit einer beliebig erfundenen Fabel stattgefunden hat. Jedenfalls muss der Kornspeicher schon zur Zeit der Entstehung des Stückes in eine Lederhalle verwandelt gewesen sein, da der Verfasser sonst wohl kaum auf den Gedanken gekommen wäre, Simon Eyre beim Könige über

---

*) Vergleiche auch das Citat aus Stowe's Survey bei Nares s. v. Rippar.

das Recht, Ledermärkte dort abhalten zu dürfen, vorstellig werden zu lassen. Leider ist es mir nicht gelungen, Stow's
grosses Werk über London zur Einsicht zu erhalten, ebenso
wenig, wie mir hier in Thorn Holinshed's Chronik zu Gebote
stand; in einem dieser Werke wird sich gewiss eine Notiz
finden, die auf den historischen Boden unseres Stückes einiges
Licht wirft.

Ueber den Verfasser des Stückes, der jedenfalls auf der
Bühne wohl zu Hause war, erlaube ich mir keine Vermuthung;
doch habe ich die Zeit der Abfassung schon im „Archiv"
B. XXVI. p. 83 näher zu bestimmen versucht und wiederhole
das dort Gesagte mit einem Zusatze. Aus der Anrede des
Prologs an die Königin (p. 5 dieses Druckes):

„Oh grant, bright mirror of true chastity
From those life-breathing stars, your sunlike eyes,
One gracious smile:"

ist wohl zu schliessen, dass das Stück schon unter der Re-
gierung Elisabeth's, die ihre Jungfräulichkeit gern preisen
hörte, entstand. Mit eben der Beziehung lässt der Dichter
wohl den Hammon in der neunten Scene (p. 25) zu Otley
von dessen Tochter sagen:

„Nay, chide her not, mylord, for doing well.
If she can live an happy virgin's life,
She is for more blessed, than to be a wife."

Diese Vermuthung wird durch die Notiz bei Collier I, 350
unterstützt, dass die Truppe Henslowe's und Edw. Alleyn's
die früher im Curtain, dann in der Fortuna spielte und sich
nach ihrem Patron Lord Nottingham's Servants nannte,
(vergl. den alten Titel p. 3) gleich nach dem Tode Elisabeth's im Jahre 1604 in den Dienst Prinz Henry's überging
und dessen Namen annahm. Es wäre zwar möglich, dass Nottingham eine neue Truppe engagirt hätte, doch findet sich
hierüber keine Nachricht. Dagegen ist bekannt, dass Elisabeth zu Weihnachten 1601 von Nottingham's Schauspielern
unterhalten wurde (Collier I, 319; vergl. 317 u. 318), womit der Anfang der Vorrede stimmt: „I present you here with
a merry conceited comedy, called ‚the shoemaker's holiday',
acted by my Lord Admiral's players at a Christmas-time
before the Queen's most excellent Majesty." Vor 1591 ist aber
das Stück auch wohl. schwerlich gespielt worden, da damals
sich erst Nottingham's Truppe bildete; auch wird (pag. 53)
des Tamburlain (vergl. Baudissin, B. Jonson u. seine
Schule p. XXIII.) und des Sultan Soliman (womit vielleicht
das Stück Soliman und Perseda, das Kyd zugeschrieben
worden ist, aus dem Jahre 1599, gemeint ist) Erwähnung gethan, so dass wir also, freilich nicht mit Sicherheit, die Abfassung des Stückes zwischen 1591 und 1603 zu setzen haben.

— Vielleicht hilft diese Zeitbestimmung, dem Dichter auf die
Spur zu kommen, für welchen die Flüchtigkeit seines Stils
characteristisch ist; z. B. hat der zweite Satz der Vorrede
(p. 3): „For the mirth and pleasant matter, by her Highness
graciously accepted, being indeed no way offensive." durch-
aus keine Construction, kann auch nicht mit dem vorhergehenden oder nachfolgenden Satze verbunden werden. Pag. 26
sagt der Lord Mayor:
>„I would have sworn, the puling girl
>Would willingly accepted Hammon's love."

wo er sagen wollte „would have accepted", oder wo die Aenderung „Would willingly accept of Hammon's love" oder „Had
willingly accepted Hammon's love" dem Verse wie dem Sinne
entsprochen hätte. Ebenso flüchtig ist mitunter der Vers ge-
baut, (z. B. p. 8: „Where honour becomes, shame attends
delay"; p. 33: „In frosty evenings, à light burning by her.")
und der Reim beobachtet, wie sich p. 39 „Jane" auf „same",
p. 41 „hate" auf „escape" reimen soll.

Was nun vorliegenden Druck anbetrifft, so hat der Her-
ausgeber die unhistorische Eintheilung in Acte für den Leser-
kreis dieser Art von Publicationen für unnöthig gehalten, doch
zur leichteren Uebersicht wenigstens die Scenen geschieden,
wobei zu bemerken ist, dass die im „Archiv" l. c. angegebene
Abtheilung sich bei näherer Prüfung als nicht ganz richtig erwiesen hat, dass Sc. 1 und 2 des Berichtes im „Archiv" in
Folge dessen in eine zusammengezogen, Sc. 4, 5, 13 und 17
in je zwei getheilt, und dadurch aus 17 Scenen deren 20 ge-
worden sind. Ausserdem ist ein Personenverzeichniss hinzu-
gefügt, der Ort der Handlung möglichst genau bestimmt, sowie hie und da eine Bühnenanweisung eingeschaltet, wie z. B.
p. 21, wo man ohne diese Zusätze (*„In a low voice"* etc.)
die Worte kaum verstehen würde. An einigen Stellen, wo
durch Beschädigung eine Lücke entstanden war, oder im Druck
eine Silbe ausgefallen schien, ist eine meist unbedeutende und
zweifellose Ergänzung vorgenommen. Alle diese Zusätze sind
durch eckige Klammern kenntlich gemacht.

Im Uebrigen habe ich mich bei der Behandlung des
Textes der Vorsicht beflissen; nur wo eine Aenderung durch-
aus geboten, und zugleich die Emendation sicher schien, ist
kurzweg geändert; z. B.

Sc. 4	p. 14	Zeile 18 v. o.	Souse-wife	in	housewife
„ 6	„ 17	„ 2 v. u.	slead	„	flayed
„ 6	„ 17	„ 1 v. u.	*Horner* (sic!)	„	*horns*
„ 10	„ 30	„ 14 v. u.	mistris	„	master
„ 10	„ 30	„ 15—17 v. o.	sind statt *Firke*, wie im		
			Original, der Frau *Eyre* zugetheilt.		
„ 20	„ 56	„ 17 v. o.	sind die Worte:		

„Fair maid this bridegroom cannot be your bride".
umgestellt in:

„This fair maid, bridegroom, cannot be your bride."

Solche Stellen, deren Sinn mir dunkel blieb, habe ich, von
der Orthographie abgesehen, die durchweg modernisirt ist, so
belassen, wie sie waren. Ich mache auf folgende besonders
aufmerksam, indem ich auch diejenigen hier gleich einrücke,
die nur eine mir unverständliche Beziehung enthalten.

Sc. 1 p. 7 Zeile 16 v. o.: wardenness; Obhut? Bereit-
schaft?

„ 1 „ 9 „ 5 v. u. und öfter: by the Lord of
Ludgate. Ist vielleicht der
Henker gemeint?

„ 1 „ 11 „ 3 v. o. und öfter: bumbast-cotton-
candle-queen (auch quean
geschrieben.)

„ 1 „ 11 „ 7 v. o.: the flower of Saint-Mar-
tin's.

„ 4 „ 14 „ 2 v. o.: powder-beef-queens.

„ 6 „ 17 „ 9 v. u. und ähnlich p. 18: Upon some,
no etc. Ist p. 18 Zeile 10 v. o.
für „I" „Ay" zu lesen?

„ 7 „ 20 „ 6 v. o.: St. Mary-Queries bells.

„ 7 „ 20 „ 1 v. u.: brown-bread tanniking.

„ 13 „ 37 „ 16 v. u.: Sib whore. cf. Nares s. v.
Sib. p. 724.

„ 15 „ 44 „ 14 v. o.: in cony. Vielleicht in cony
(cf. Nares s. v., p. 400), was
aber auch keinen rechten Sinn
giebt.

„ 17 „ 50 „ 9 v. o.: good laced mutton. Nares'
Erklärung dieser sonst nicht sel-
tenen Redensart passt hier nicht.
Auch soll wohl ein Wortspiel mit
dem vorhergehenden „Lacy"
darin liegen.

Ausser diesen Stellen sind, namentlich in den zum Theil
absichtlich verdrehten Reden Eyre's und Sibyl's, manche andere, die noch der Erklärung bedürfen, oder auch vielleicht gar
keinen Sinn haben, wie auch in andern Sprachen manche
Scherzworte, Flüche und Mode-Redensarten. Wenn Firke
Sc. 7 p. 21 von einem Schiffe erzählt „of silk cypress, laden
with sugar-candy" so soll dies wohl komische Wortversetzung
sein, in Stelle von „a ship of Cyprus and Candy, laden with
silk and sugar." Die Bezeichnung „Doctor Commons" statt
„Doctors' Commons" Sc. 2 p. 12 soll im Munde Sibyl's gewiss ihre niedrige Sprache characterisiren. — Nicht corrigirt

ist Manches, was sonst als Fehler gälte, aus ähnlichen Grün-
den; z. B. Sc. 17 p. 48 „these humble weeds makes thee
more beautiful" etc., da sich diese Licenz auch in Shakespear (Rom. and Jul. II, 3, Note 16, Macb. II, 1, Note 32
bei Delius) vorfindet; sie kehrt in unserm Stück Sc. 17,
p. 51 wieder: „tarts and custards comes quavering in malt-
shovels." Auch Anderes blieb unverändert, wenn irgend eine
Möglichkeit vorhanden war, z. B. ein adjectivisches „nimbly"
Sc. 19 p. 52, statt „nimble," welches sich p. 53 findet.

Zur vollständigen Erklärung des Stückes würde eine ge-
naue Kenntniss von Handwerksgebräuchen, sowie der Londoner
Stadtgeschichte und Topographie gehören. Für deutsche Leser
bemerke ich nur Folgendes: Oldford existirt noch heute, freilich innerhalb, nicht mehr ausserhalb der Stadt, hinter Beth-
nal-Green, am Regent's Canal. Die St. Faith's Church
„under St. Paul's" (p. 44) ist eine Krypte unter der St. Pauls-
kirche, und eine der ältesten in London. The Savoy (p. 44)
ist die noch vorhandene Capelle des abgebrochenen Savoy
Palace, Strand, nahe Waterloo Bridge. Ueber den Pissing
Conduit (ib.) giebt Nares p. 595 Auskunft. Tuttlefields
(p. 7) ist dasselbe, was sonst gewöhnlich Tothill-fields hiess,
ehemals ein Platz ausserhalb der Stadt; jetzt giebt es nur noch
zwei Tothill Streets in Westminster, hinter der Abtei,
südlich von St. James' Park. cf. Nares s. v. Tuttle, p. 835.
Schenken zum Schwan (p. 19) gab es damals zwei, „The swan
at Dowgate, a tavern well known" und „the swan" in Old-Fish-
Street; beide, so weit ich dies ermitteln kann, nicht allzu weit
von Towerstreet, wo Eyre's Haus ist. (Vergl. Drake II,
133, Note.) — Die Pancake-bell hat den Namen von
Pfannkuchen, die man schon damals am Fastelabend (Shrove-
tuesday oder Pancake-tuesday) in England gegessen
hat. Dieser Tag war „a day of holiday andlicence for apprentices, labouring persons and others" (Nares s. v. Shroving
p. 723). Ebenso der vorhergehende Collop-Monday. Man
nannte collops (p. 51) im Norden Englands Fleischschnitte,
welche den Winter hindurch gesalzen und getrocknet waren.
Der Fastendinstag wurde durch die pancake-bell einge-
läutet, über welche der „Water-poet" Taylor, erzählt:
„Shrove-Tuesday, at whose entrance in the morning all the
whole kingdom is unquiet, but by that time the clock strikes
eleven, which (by the help of a knavish sexton) is commonly
before nine, then there is a bell rung, called pancake-bell,
the sound whereof makes thousands of people distracted, and
forgetful either of manners or humanity." Besonders die Hand-
werkslehrlinge und Gesellen betrachteten diesen Tag als ihren
speciellen Feiertag und machten mancherlei Unfug, indem sie
eine Art von Polizei ausübten. Vergl. Drake, I, 141 ff.

7

Diese Strassenjustiz der Gesellen, die auch der Lord Mayor gelegentlich bei Aufläufen anrief, kommt auch bei Shakespear vor: Henry VIII; V, 3; Henry VI, erster Theil, I, 3 am Schluss, wenn daselbst nicht besondere mit Keulen bewaffnete Officianten gemeint sind. — St. Hugh erscheint, ich weiss nicht warum, in dem ganzen Stücke (auch in dem zweiten Threemen's song (p. 4) als Schutzpatron der Schuhmacher, und St. Hugh's bones (p. 15) sollen der Knochen sein, dessen sich auch heute noch die Schuhmacher zum Glätten bedienen. — Was Nares p. 308 über den St. Georges' day sagt, wird gut erläutert durch die Stelle Sc. 17 p. 48, wo der Diener mit „blue-coat" angeredet wird. Uebrigens pflegten Bediente gewöhnlich blaue Röcke zu tragen. Drake II, 138. Auch andere Erklärungen in Nares werden durch Stellen unseres Stückes belegt, und umgekehrt, z. B. mealy mouth Sc. 1, p. 9, uplandish Sc. 4 p. 15, clubs for prentices Sc. 17, p. 47. Vergleiche auch die Note p. 59. Der Dichter hat die Bestallung des Lord-Mayors, welche auf Simonis und Judae Tag fiel (Ende October) mit dichterischer Freiheit auf den Shrove-tuesday verlegt. Ueber die dabei gebräuchliche Feierlichkeit giebt Drake , 162 ff. Auskunft. Ich bemerke nur, dass die „company" des Lordmayors (p. 52) die Innung ist, zu der er gehört, und dass der ebendaselbst erwähnte Umstand, dass die Mitglieder seiner Innung, in eine bestimmte Tracht gekleidet, bei der Einführungs-Ceremonie den Lord Mayor und seinen Gästen aufwarten, ebenfalls historisch ist. Bei Drake l. c. sagt ein Zeitgenosse hierüber: Darauf kommen (in dem Zuge durch die City) „the bachelors two and two together, in long gowns, with crimson hoods on their shoulders of satin; which bachelors are chosen every year of the same company that the Mayor is of, (but not of the livery,) and serve as gentlemen on that and other festival days; to wait on the Mayor" etc. In welchem Verhältnisse aber „livery" zu „company" stand, vermag ich nicht anzugeben; (none but the livery of my company shall wait upon etc., sagt Eyre l. c., vergl. die eben citirte Stelle: the same company that the Mayor is of (but not of the same livery).). — Dass Roger Sc. 10, p. 28 Mrs. Eyre eine Pfeife Taback anbietet, ist nicht auffällig, da damals auch viele Frauen rauchten. Siehe Drake II, 137.

Die meisten Schwierigkeiten machten die zahlreichen plattdeutschen Stellen in den Scenen 4, 7, 10, 11, 13, 14. Offenbar hat der Dichter nur sehr mangelhaft den Dialect verstanden, den er hat schreiben wollen, der Setzer hat das Seinige zur Entstellung gethan, so dass man manchmal nicht weiss, ob die Worte englisch oder deutsch sein sollen. Wahrscheinlich soll der vlämische oder geldersche Dialect nachgeahmt sein. Was daran durch Vereinfachung der Orthographie und

'eine Nachhülfen zu bessern war, habe ich gethan, s
‘ geändert, so dass eine beträchtliche Menge von ,.
  r die ich keinen Rath weiss. Vielleicht, dass Andere
  ..uerer Kenntniss jener Dialecte noch manches Wort zu
..ren und zu emendiren vermögen. Namentlich mache ich
..fmerksam auf:

Sc. 4 p. 15 Zeile 5 v. o.: Upsolce se byen.

„ 7 „ 19. „ 11 v. u.: lot det sign vn swannekin.
Der Sinn ist freilich klar, aber
ich weiss keine sich eng an-
schliessende Emendation.

„ 7 „ 22 „ 22 v. o.: De skip been in rouere.
Vielleicht in Dover oder the
road.

„ 11 „ 32 „ 23 v. u.: good frister.

„ 13 „ 37 „ 4 v. u.: Vat begaie gon vat vod gon
frister?

„ „ „ „ „ 1 v. u.: egl?, soll wohl edle heissen.

„ 14 „ 40 „ 8 v. u.: it fall vel out (velout ist
ein. ruckfehler.)

Von emendirten Stellen dieser Art bemerke ich:

Sc. 4 p. 16 Zeile 2 v. o.: for to mask. Im Original
steht voour mask.

„ 7 „ 19 „ 18 v. u.: all voll statt alwoll.

„ L3 „ 36 „ 4 v. u.: vamps; oder vampers? Das
Original hat vanpres.

www.ingramcontent.com/pod-product-compliance
Lightning Source LLC
Chambersburg PA
CBHW031245260626
47169CB00007B/2456